Kangazang!
small cosmos

TERRY COOPER

CANDY JAR BOOKS · CARDIFF
2025

The right of Terry Cooper to be identified as the
Author of the Work has been asserted by him in accordance
with the Copyright, Designs and Patents Act 1988.

Copyright © Terry Cooper 2018/25

Editor: Will Rees
Cover: Terry Cooper
Editorial: Keren Williams & Shaun Russell

Printed and bound in the UK by
4edge, 22 Eldon Way, Hockley, Essex, SS5 4AD

ISBN: 978-1-912535-27-9

Published by
Candy Jar Books
Mackintosh House
136 Newport Road, Cardiff, CF24 1DJ
www.candyjarbooks.co.uk

To Colin Baker,
Hayley Cox, Yoss Nutt,
Will Rees, Andy Frankham-Allen

And everyone who bought and read
the first two *KANGAZANG!* books,

This is for you.

And as ever,
Douglas Adams.

prologue

Worry. Don't Be Happy.

'As a rule, men worry more about what they can't see than about what they can.'
Julius Caesar

Ray the Barber climbed into the pilot seat of the Marshmallow Penguin and set a course for home. The little spaceship flew down towards Kangazang's mottled pink and yellow surface, breaking through the clouds like a flea emerging from the fleece of a sheep for a spot of fresh air.

Something was very wrong. And not just with that metaphor.

No moving traffic on the ground, in the sea, or in the air. Nobody on the beaches or the streets. The ship flew past Galavantia Central Spaceport, and it was deserted too. For a planet entirely dedicated to fun and leisure, the place was eerily quiet.

Ray attempted to contact the landing authority by radio: Silence. He tried the music channels: Nothing. The ship's computer yielded zilch as well: The InfoHexNet was quieter than a mute swan with its beak glued shut, sulking.

Everyone on board looked at each other in confusion with a large side helping of fear. Ray scratched his beard and looked over at his father sitting beside him, hoping for a suggestion as to what to do next. Col just shrugged, equally clueless. Behind him, Jeff Spooner and his robotic girlfriend, Tailback, sat in stunned silence.

Suddenly, a cold, authoritative voice came over the ship's speakers:

'Attention, Marshmallow Penguin! This is the Macadamian Dictatorship. We are now in complete control of the population of Kangazang! You will obey every command, and will land immediately or be shot down. This is not negotiable!'

The four occupants of the ship gasped in perfect harmony.

'Oh my Bod,' said Ray. 'Not those nutjobs again!'

'An invasion?' said Jeff.

'Not negotiable?' said Col.

'This is terrible!' said Tailback. 'Not now!'

'I know!' said Jeff. 'I'm a bit knackered for an invasion right this minute, as it happens!'

'No, you don't understand!' said Tailback. 'I think I'm about to give birth!'

The ship took a steep dive as Ray momentarily lost the feeling in all of his limbs.

Tailback's revelation was a shock to Ray for two reasons: Firstly, he'd had no knowledge of any activities of the hanky-panky variety going on between her and his best friend, the Earthman Jeff Spooner, and secondly, Tailback was an android. Not a cyborg, but a completely

2

artificial life form from the planet Orbitron. Jeff, the Earthman, kebab addict and recent intergalactic adventurer, and his girlfriend, Tailback, a female android... It's a long story. Like, two novels long.

Tailback stared at her abdomen cavity, which was fizzing and glowing orange as if someone had filled her up with orangeade and popped a few mints in for giggles. But no one was giggling; in fact, Jeff was rapidly turning a shade of pale hitherto undiscovered. Ray's father, Col, looked on in utter astonishment and with just a little awkwardness – after all, this phenomenon was partly his doing. Tailback had sought him out, desperately seeking a way to become able to bear children, and Col had had just the thing – a box of nanobots that he'd smuggled out from her home planet of Orbitron, and which, if given the right molecular ingredients to work with, could be programmed to construct a child. One of Jeff's tears had become that vital ingredient, and so now the child was being constructed – and at astonishing speed. It was half human, half Orbot, fused together at a molecular level. A perfect hybrid entity, the like of which had never been seen before. Fascinating, unlimited potential. Truly unique.

And then Jeff had gone and sneezed on it, imprinting it with the name 'ErHuer'.

chapter one

Gonna Give You Up, Gonna Let You Down,
Gonna Run Around and Desert You

*'The other night I ate at a real family restaurant.
Every table had an argument going.'*
George Carlin

R ay spotted a number of Macadamian interceptor
ships on the horizon, closing in fast.

'I don't know what's happening back there,' he called
over his shoulder to his friends. 'But we're about to be
captured! Hang onto something!'

'Never mind that,' Jeff hollered back, 'my bird's
about to drop a sprog! Can't we lose 'em or
something?'

Col and Tailback looked at each other: Nothing
remotely sausage-like.

'No!' yelled Ray. 'We're almost out of power! More
to the point—'

A loud bang shook the ship. Sparks rained down on the
frightened crew, and smoke bellowed out of vents. Red lights
lit up and sirens did sirenny things. Ray hit the autopilot

4

button and rolled out of the pilot's seat onto the floor. He crawled over to the huddled group.

'Er, they're armed too,' he added.

Col raised an eyebrow. 'What makes you say that, son?'

'We're all going to die!' wailed Jeff, characteristically feebly.

'No, we're not,' said Col, trying to remain positive.

'We probably are, in all honesty, Dad,' said Ray, trying to remain paranoid.

Jeff covered his face with his hands. 'Do something, Ray!' he pleaded.

'I am! I'm shaking as fast as I can!'

'I'm too young to die,' burbled Jeff, clinging onto Tailback's hand. 'I read that book about a hundred and one things to do before you die, and I haven't done any of 'em!'

'You mean you haven't even swum with dolphins?' said Ray.

Jeff thought for a moment.

'Do trout count?'

'Near enough,' said Ray. 'You can die happy now.'

Suddenly Jeff began yelping in pain.

'It's shrapnel!' yelled Ray.

'It's whiplash!' yelled Col.

'It's Tailback!' yelled Jeff. 'She's breaking my hand!'

Tailback was having the robotic equivalent of contractions. She tensed up and grimaced as the still-fizzing child inside her kept growing. Suddenly, a couple of her stomach plates popped off their mountings, and the child, the size of a basketball, rolled out onto the deck.

Jeff let go of Tailback's promptly relaxed hand and jumped back, staring in terror at the sparkling sphere. Tailback looked at him.

'It's all right, Jeff. He's fine. It's all over.'

'Eh? Really? For who?' said Jeff in bewilderment.

They all sat around the infant, staring in silent amazement as it uncurled and stretched its limbs.

Childbirth is a pretty bewildering experience for anyone, but probably a few hundred times more bizarre when the child in question is a sparkling silver proto-cyborg. There was no crying, no umbilical cord – nothing more to do except pick it up and check it was functioning. Ray looked back at the cockpit and saw that the interceptor ships had positioned themselves in front of the Marshmallow Penguin, preventing any escape attempt. He got up and took the pilot seat again, followed by his father, who had seen enough craziness for one day.

Tailback gently picked up the baby-ball-thing and stood, helped by Jeff.

'Wow, is it really our baby?' whispered Jeff tenderly. Despite the strangeness of the situation, he was enthralled by the prospect of becoming a dad, although he had no inkling that he was a first in the universe – the father of a true molecular cyborg. It had never been done before. This was no mere LoBorg, cobbled together primitively, with a plastic foot and a metal skull. This was something else.

Clean and a metallic colour, it was neither metal nor plastic, nor flesh, but a sort of semi-organic putty through which pulsed tiny beads of light. Tailback passed the baby over to Jeff so that he could hold his child for the first time. Jeff nearly dropped it. It was much heavier than its size suggested. Whatever material it was made of, it must have been very dense. The baby vibrated ever so softly at his touch.

'We're parents, Jeff,' said Tailback nervously. 'Can you believe it?'

'Oh, come 'ere, love!' said Jeff, throwing an arm around the pretty Orbot. 'I've never been happier. What's not to like? I've got you, you've got me, and we've got our little... man here. Er... it is a boy, then?'

'Yes. He was designated male by your organic contribution.'

'Er... my what now?' said Jeff, feeling a tad embarrassed.

'Your teardrop. It contained your DNA.'

'Oh, I see. That's a relief.'

'I think we should feed him now,' said Tailback.

Jeff scratched his head, looking around.

'Er, yeah. What do you think he eats though? I mean, I don't suppose you've got any, erm... you know... milk, somewhere?'

'Might be some in the fridge,' said Ray.

Jeff looked at Col.

' 'Ere, you gave her the ability to have kids. Did you perhaps give her, um... y'know?'

'No, I most certainly did not!' said Col.

'Power and data,' said Tailback. 'That is all he'll need. He won't consume very much at this size.'

'You can tell that?' asked Jeff. 'I suppose it's mother's intuition?'

Tailback tilted her head. 'It's not that. I can... feel his thoughts inside my main processing unit. I can detect his emotions and his state of mind.'

Jeff blinked. Which was what he often liked to do when he had no idea what to think.

'You mean... like telepathy?'

'Wi-Fi.'

'Oh, OK. I reckon we can get the little lad some grub

from the ship. Think we can plug him into this socket, here?' He indicated a square panel on the ship's inner hull. Tailback opened the panel and pulled out a thin cable with a rectangular plug on the end.

'Will that, er... fit?' said Jeff.

'Universal Serial Bus,' said Tailback.

Jeff smiled at the realisation that 'universal' really did mean that.

Tailback connected the baby to the cable and gently placed him inside the hull cavity, where he glowed contentedly, feeding on the power and data that streamed from the ship's computer core.

'He'll be happy enough there for now,' said Tailback.

'Fairy nuff, I s'pose,' said Jeff. With a start he remembered the Macadamians. 'Hey, what's happening outside?'

Everyone headed for the cockpit in a state of deceptively internalised panic.

'What's the score then, Ray?' asked Jeff.

'One-nil to the Macadamian Dictators, Jeff. We're stuffed. They've got us banged to lefts.'

'What? Have they really taken over the entire planet?'

Col nodded. 'Afraid so. While we were running around the galaxy fighting a war with our mad ex-girlfriends, they infiltrated every level of administration and seized control of Kangazang. We've had no choice but to surrender or be blown to bits.'

'Oh my gawd,' moaned Jeff.

'But you helped them, Ray!' said Tailback. 'Didn't you get them a meeting with the government? To set them up as a planetary defence force?'

'They seemed genuine enough at the time,' said Ray

dolefully. 'How was I to know they were only playing dumb to get their foot in the door?'

'Oh, bugger,' said Jeff. 'So what now?'

He was answered by a new announcement over the ship's radio.

'Now you will accompany us and land immediately. Any attempt to escape or deviate from this course will result in instant smashification by laser.'

'Suppose we'd better do as we're told then!' said Ray, grabbing the steering and setting course for the surface of Kangazang.

Ah! New tales, new arrivals, new dangers. All new, folks! Talking of which, I feel I should introduce myself. Why? Because I'm not who you thought I was, that's why.

My name is Gridlock. Or to be more formal, M4. Or to be less formal, Grid. I'm assuming that by now you know who and what I am, but for those nutjobs who jump into an epic trilogy at the final part, I'd better quickly refresh your memory circuits.

I'm an Orbot, just like Tailback. An artificial life form, created on – and by – the computer world of Orbitron. Tailback is my sister, for want of a more accurate term. We met up with Jeff and Ray when they once made a pit-stop on Orbitron for repairs and we sort of… stowed away.

You see, my sister – originally named 'M25', but renamed 'Tailback' by Jeff – and I are designated 'M' Class. This means we have certain personality defects that prevent us from being perfect members of Orbot society. I have this rather strange tendency to find things three hundred percent funnier than they're meant to be, and Tailback had what you humans would call 'phobias'. Unfortunately, her phobias would change every few minutes. The mega-mainframes of Orbitron soon became a little impatient with my laughing and her screaming. So much so that they stamped us with an 'M' for 'Malfunction' and dumped us up on the surface where we couldn't annoy them. Poor Tailback found it terrifying. I laughed my plastic bottom off, as you can imagine.

Since fleeing Orbitron, we've both found that personality defects such as ours aren't that uncommon among humans, and for me at least, it's become something of a marketable skill: I'm now the galaxy's highest paid stand-up comedian without even trying to be – it just sort of comes naturally to me. I once said to Jeff that I would retire if I could no longer hear the sound of laughter. He said, 'That's never stopped you before.' Jealousy is a terrible thing.

Anyway, I'm doing rather well. And look – I'm a novelist now! Hah! Priceless! My sister, Tailback, has had a somewhat different journey. She's been cured of her phobias – awfully long story, I won't bore you – and fallen in love with Jeff. Clumsy of her, I know. Then they fell out, now they've fallen back in and had a baby.

Which brings me back to... well, me again. The reason I'm taking over the task of chronicling this third and final part of the tale of Jeff Spooner is that ErHuer, the sweet little baby that we just met (and your narrator up to this point) isn't able to continue. Without giving too much away, let's just say that I've got a slightly less involved role in the proceedings from here on in, and a clearer recollection of events. You'll understand more as we go. Or maybe you won't. But make like a band-aid and stick around, because it gets better. Hah! Priceless!

So, where was I… Oh yeah, the invasion of Kangazang, I hear you ask? Well, at the time, I was looking after Ray's beach house down on the surface, preparing for my new planet-wide comedy tour, entitled 'Hilarity to Ten Decimal Places', when the entirety of Galavantia City was taken captive by the Macadamian forces. These short, nut-based life forms came to Kangazang a few months ago, with the aim of invading the planet, and all because of some age-old prophecy. Luckily, Ray outwitted them (temporarily, it seems) and persuaded them to take it easy and peacefully co-exist with the Kangazanian people. Unfortunately, as we have seen, this didn't last long. Nutters. In every sense.

When the occupation began, I did what any upstanding, proud citizen would do and thought about defending my home from the invaders. Then I remembered that I wasn't an actual citizen and was therefore exempt from heroics of any sort. I did what any upstanding coward would do: I quickly disassembled myself and hid in the cupboard under the sink.

Anyway, moving on…

The *Marshmallow Penguin*, escorted by three Macadamian interceptor craft, touched down on the landing platform of the now-deserted Galavantia Central Spaceport. Inside, Jeff, Ray, Col and Tailback peered out of the portholes to see their captors arranging themselves into a circle around the little silver ship.

'Hasn't anyone thought of a plan yet?' Jeff asked. It was his way of admitting that he hadn't himself.

'Well, let's do what we usually do,' said Ray, putting on his white barber's coat and trying to look composed in the face of certain doom.

'Yeah. Good one, matey, let's... Erm, what *do* we usually do then?'

'Doesn't it involve crying, bickering and surrender, in some fashion?' asked Col, trying his utmost to remain impartial.

Ray felt he had to agree, but also felt this was not the time to admit it.

'Not this time, Dad. Come on, let's go and see what these nutcases want.'

'And I'll do the talking, all right, mate?' said Jeff indignantly. 'You practically gave them the key to the city last time!'

'I might have. But where were you at the time, Action Jeff? Oh, I remember – running away, leaving me to fend for myself, as I recall.'

Tailback looked back and forth between Jeff and Ray, then to Col.

'There's the bickering part,' said Col, shrugging. Tailback sighed.

Ray went over to the entry hatch, huffing in frustration.

Jeff suddenly remembered that he was a parent, and, as such, had others to consider.

' 'Ang a banger! What about the baby?'

'Oh yes,' said Ray. 'Bring him along. Can't very well leave him here.'

'Yes, actually, I think we can,' said Tailback, rather unexpectedly.

'You sure, love?' asked Jeff. 'You haven't got a touch of the post-natal depressions, have you?'

'No, Jeff, I'm functioning at optimal levels,' replied the pretty Orbot, wrapping her overcoat around her exposed midsection. 'He's feeding. If they scan the ship, he won't show up as a life form, and he'll be safe.'

'Oh. Well, OK, but only if you're sure.'

'He'll be downloading system updates for a while. I'm tuned into his brainwaves, remember? And he's tuned into mine. I should be able to detect if he's in any trouble.'

She gently placed the cover back over the cavity, hiding the newborn as he suckled on the ship's power feed and installed Service Pack Three.

Ray pushed the ship's hatch open and stepped out hesitantly, followed by Col, Jeff and Tailback. They descended the ramp and stood among the group of squat Macadamian soldiers, each one tooled up with fearsome-looking weapons.

Dressed in their traditional battle armour, which quite fittingly looked like nut shells, the Macadamians were identical. Their shiny brown heads displayed no differentiation, and they shared the same single-minded grimace. Clearly, they were not in any mood for fun. Unless said fun involved blowing people away with guns.

'Hello, chaps!' said Ray brightly, in the hope that pleasantries would be the order of the day. His hopes were swiftly dashed on the rocks of abruptness, as one of the nut-soldiers stepped forward and pulled out his radio device.

'Shellshock calling Pistachio One... Shellshock calling Pistachio One. Have captured one human, two natives and an Orbot. Advise, please.'

The little chap waited a moment then the reply came back, presumably from Pistachio One, whatever that was.

13

'Shellshock, this is Pistachio One. Bring them in for interrogation. The Big Nut wants to see them.'

The soldier signed off and pointed his weapon at Ray.

'Right! You lot get moving! The colonel wants to see you. Move it!'

Ray put his hands up in a show of servility.

'Colonel? Is that Colonel Kernel? We've met. I know him! He'll sort all this out, just you wait!'

Jeff joined in. Enthusiastic pleading was one of his specialties.

'Yeah! We're old mates! This is just all one almighty cock-up!'

The soldier jumped in shock at Jeff's sudden input, reflexively blasting him with a stun bolt. Right in the sensitives.

Jeff squeaked, collapsing to the ground as gracefully as a sack of porridge. The soldier pointed the way forward again.

'No more talk! Get moving. And someone pick that up!' he barked, pointing to Jeff.

Tailback effortlessly pulled her sensation-free boyfriend up off the concrete and slung him over her shoulder, where he proceeded to drool saliva down the back of her leg.

In the capital city square stood the impressive Palace of Kangazang.

The palace was a masterpiece of Kangazanian architecture: late Zing dynasty, thrusting out multi-coloured spires and psychedelic-coloured stone ramparts in all directions. It looked like an explosion in a crayon factory, decorated by colour blind chimpanzees. Dali would've derided it for being too silly; Jackson Pollock would've said it was a bit messy.

There was no monarchy to occupy it, more of a casual government with no rivals to oppose them. In fact there was only one party – and that was the kind involving a punch bowl and loud music. Most people on the quirky holiday world of Kangazang were only there to relax, have fun and take it easy, not get bogged down in boring politics. As if there is any other kind.

But now the palace played host to the Dictators of Macadamia, an ancient protein-based race, long ridiculed for their almost maniacal dedication to an age old prophecy that basically told them to go out there and conquer anything they came into contact with.

Why so hostile? This would show the people of the galaxy that they were not to be taken with a pinch of salt. Pun intended. In short (additional pun intended), they had a severe case of 'short man syndrome' – they overcompensated with machismo and aggression just because they looked so tiny and cute.

As the group entered the main hall, they saw the diminutive figure of Colonel Kernel, the commander in chief of the Macadamian forces, sitting on the antique lilac throne at the far end of the room.

Although he wanted to burst out laughing at the sight of a two-foot tall peanut sitting on a throne, Jeff had only recently awoken with what was, to him, a familiar throbbing headache. So he elected to remain quiet. It was one of those rare occasions when he had a sensible idea.

The prisoners stopped in front of the throne and watched as Colonel Kernel tried his best to glare menacingly while wobbling on four small cushions. Ray stifled a snigger. Col bit his lip, tears in his eyes, and even Tailback blinked in disbelief with a hand over her mouth unit. Jeff was still feeling a trifle dizzy and sensibly did nothing. He already knew the pain of being hit in the unmentionables with a stun bolt and was not going to volunteer for another taste. Not on yours, his or anyone else's nelly.

'Hello there. Colonel Kernel, isn't it?' said Ray.

'Barbaray Sprambladack Fasstalon-Scump! You remember me then?' said the colonel triumphantly.

Ray shrugged.

'I never forget a face. But in your case, I'd be happy to make an exception. Listen, what's this all about, eh? I thought you lot were having fun here, not preparing to invade!'

'Aha! Well, that fooled you, didn't it? We're not easily dissuaded. We're onto all the tall man's tricks. Thought you could have us serving the people of Kangazang, did you? Well, think again! We're a race of rulers! Dictators! We stand tall, allowing no one to look down on us!'

Col coughed to hide a chuckle. Ray elbowed him to stop it.

'But, Colonel,' said Ray, 'you didn't need to go and invade the place! This is a peaceful planet! People come and go as they please. It was fine as it was. What have you got to gain from this madness?'

The colonel grabbed his swagger stick – a short rod with a golden ball at one end that he used to keep his troops marching in time – and directed it at Ray's beard.

'That's precisely it, Scump! Madness! We know what the vertically over-privileged think of us! You think we're mad! That we don't possess the drive, the courage, ambition or sense to rule! Well, let me tell you this: We're not mad, we're not stupid and we're not nuts!'

He paused for a moment.

'Well, we ARE nuts, obviously. But we're not crazy!'

At that point, the colonel's waving of his stick made him overbalance. The cushions provided no security. He fell off the throne, bouncing and rolling onto the floor at the feet of his prisoners.

Ray smirked and his father elbowed him back. This nutty Napoleon had finally cracked. The Colonel jumped to his feet in an 'I-meant-to-do-that-actually' kind of way, scraping together as much dignity as he could. He strolled over to a small podium, upon which sat a silver projection box. He paused momentarily, waiting as one of his subordinates ran over with a box for him to stand on. Tailback flinched, holding in a giggle, and both Ray and Col's shoulders began to jiggle as the colonel struggled to climb up onto it. Jeff bit his lip very hard as the tears of laughter started to well up in his eyes.

The colonel flicked the power switch, and a holographic map floated above the podium, its neon shapes and spheres swirling around in the air. The colonel pointed his stick up at the map, and a large number of tiny beige flags began to pop up all over the place.

'We've taken over this entire galactic sector! Not just Kangazang, but its neighbouring planets – look: Felyxx, Laurandishax, Chrysanthemus, Mikibrix, Jupitus and Tesko. And the rest! All under Macadamian rule! Now tell me we're useless!'

Ray had given up appealing to this tiny tin-pot dictator. Col stepped up in his place.

'Colonel, nobody has ever said anything of the sort!

We can all see you're a great leader, in command of an impressive army. But hostility and invasion aren't the way to greatness. You're fighting a war against your own paranoia. Nobody opposes you!'

The colonel hopped off his box and paced around his captive audience, quickly getting a crick in his neck from looking up at them.

'No, not now. Now they see us for our might, our determination and resolve! Our empire has begun to spread. Soon we will claim our place in history as the supreme power in the universe!'

Jeff was aching, tired and concerned for his son. This wasn't the first megalomaniacal nutjob that he'd had to listen to since he left Earth. And they were all the same: Wildly insane, with little regard for common sense, logic or goodwill. Colonel Kernel fit the profile: Hitler, Napoleon, Amin, Hussein, Caesar and Cowell. Nutters, the lot of them.

'Blimey,' said Jeff, 'I've always said, never trust a midget – their brains are too close to their arses.'

'I know exactly what you are capable of,' continued the colonel, not seeming to have heard. 'I watched as you defeated the Queen of the Slargs out there in orbit. So I'm securing you under lock and key, where I can keep my eye on you.'

Everyone noticed the irony. The colonel had no chance of getting up to eye-level with anyone – not without some kind of ladder anyway. The group began to snigger as quietly as they could manage.

Colonel Kernel directed his soldiers to move the captives on. The henchmen trotted up and jostled the group away, poking them in their legs like sheepdogs nipping at uncooperative sheep.

'Take them to the prison camps!' ordered the colonel, climbing up onto his stack of cushions. 'Watch them closely. Make them work hard and beat them regularly!'

Jeff was terrified; he hadn't worked hard for years.

The guards steered Jeff, Ray, Col and Tailback out of the throne room and down corridor after corridor, silent save for the echo of the footsteps, which, fittingly, sounded like someone munching on a mouthful of peanuts. As they passed turnings and doorways, everyone silently considered making a run for it. But it was no use. Not all of them would make it, and those who didn't would get blasted. So they remained quiet and dutiful, waiting for an opportunity to discuss a plan of action. In the meantime, everyone was glad enough just to be away from the bonkers little nut.

The shell-clad miniature militia marched the group out of the palace through the rear doors, into a large garden area usually reserved for formal functions. In front of them, waiting on the landing pad, was a Macadamian shuttle craft. It was a smaller version of their main ships: A light brown, organic shape with numerous dimples all over it. The Macadamians had a natural affinity for the shape and form of the humble peanut, it has to be said.

Jeff watched as the shell-ship opened up a small hatch on its side. It was going to be an uncomfortable ride; despite their impressive takeover of Kangazang and its surrounding planets, the Macadamian Dictators had not made allowances for any prisoners who happened to be taller than themselves. Which was basically everyone.

In fact, during their millennia-long existence, the Macadamians had only come across one race that they towered over, and that was the incredibly densely compressed inhabitants of a giant mega-planet named Skwott. These people were small in stature only because of their home planet's gravity, which was many times that of a standard, Earth-like sphere. With great gravity comes great strength, and in the end, the Skwottians kicked the peanut butter out of the Macadamian invaders. It was a painful, vicious battle, but more importantly, incredibly embarrassing: it's not every empire that gets sent packing by a bunch of angry gnomes. That episode alone put their plans for galactic domination back a few centuries.

Inside the shuttle craft, Jeff and Ray sat hunched up in seats that felt like they had been taken from an infants' school. As soon as Tailback and Col had squeezed in alongside them, the door was sealed and the ship lifted off.

Col reached across and tapped Jeff on his shoulder.

'Listen,' he said in a cautious whisper, 'I have an escape plan.'

'Really? What's that then?' asked Jeff.

'Open the door and jump out,' said Col, pointing at the hatch.

Jeff turned back to Ray and sighed.

'Kangazang... '

'What about it?' said Ray.

'Not renowned for its great thinkers, is it?'

Col tapped Jeff on the shoulder again.

'I heard that!'

'I know. You're as nutty as this lot. How do you think we'd survive that?'

'These are paratroopers,' said Col, nodding at the

backs of the Macadamian troops. 'They jump out of these things all the time. There must be parachutes around here somewhere!'

'I know what you're saying, mate,' said Jeff, 'but I can't see any parachutes hanging around the gaff. More to the point, if there were any, they'd be the size of hankies, wouldn't they?'

'Still, worth a try...' said Col, summoning up superhuman reserves of optimism.

'Suicide is *not* worth a try,' said Jeff flatly.

Ray leaned over with a pained grunt.

'He does have a point, Dad. I've seen these chaps in action. They just jump out and hit the ground running. Literally. Shells, you see. No parachutes.'

'Any more brilliant ideas, oh great Guru?' said Jeff.

Col grunted in indignation and looked away.

Jeff sat back and sighed.

'Come on, Jeff,' said Ray, 'don't be like that. At least he's trying to think of something.'

'Trying is the operative word, matey.'

Tailback, ever the logical one, had been processing all the variables and options open to them. Which didn't take long, as there weren't many. In fact there were so few, it hardly required the mind of a highly complex android. It wouldn't even have needed Stephen Hawking. Truth be told, it could probably have been handled by Steven Seagal.

Tailback had come up with a solution that was just like her: Logical, practical and just a little bit mad.

'Let me do it. I'll jump out.'

Jeff wasn't drinking anything, but he still spluttered and choked nonetheless. Ray wished Jeff *had* been drinking something, as then he would've been sprayed with something other than saliva.

'Are you serious, love? You'll never withstand the fall!'

'Correct, Jeff.'

'You'll be smashed to bits!' added Ray, helpfully.

'So that's that then,' said Jeff decisively. 'You're not going anywhere. We all stay here and see where they take us. Right?'

'Wrong,' said Tailback. 'Look after Jeff for me. I'll be back as soon as I can.'

Before Jeff, Col or Ray had time to process what the pretty Orbot had said, she had rammed her palm into the door's lock, forcing it open. She dived out of the shuttle, curling up into a ball as she fell, tumbling down to the surface of Kangazang.

'Tail! No!' cried Jeff over his spilt milk.

Ray grabbed his arm.

'It's no use. She's gone!'

A soldier trotted down the aisle to check what the commotion was. Seeing the hatch wide open, filling the shuttle with torrents of whirling air, he pointed his stun gun at Col.

'You! Hairy human! Close that door at once!'

Col grabbed the hatch door and pulled it shut. The soldier sniggered.

'Hah! You humans – always arguing and fighting! Can't just agree to disagree, can you? Someone always has to get thrown out the airlock.'

Jeff, tears of rage in his eyes, dived at the smug little soldier.

'That was my bird, you little tosspot!'

The soldier lifted his stun gun and squeezed the trigger, but Jeff had got hold of it, pushing it upwards. As it discharged its electron pulse, it was in contact with the soldier's forehead. The guard stiffened and collapsed, faint trails of smoke coming from his body.

Ray and Col looked at the smoking corpse then back at each other.

'You've killed him!' gasped Ray.

'Is it wrong to say that it actually smells rather nice?' said Col.

Jeff stared at the body, still seething with anger, tears rolling down his cheeks.

'I'm not stopping there,' he growled. 'It's time someone fought back. I've had all I can take of this lot.'

Five more soldiers bounded into the holding area, brandishing their weapons. Their commander pointed to Jeff.

'This one. He murdered the guard. No incarceration for you now. The sentence is death!'

The five guards zapped the three remaining prisoners into unconsciousness.

Our plastic princess, Tailback, was also unconscious. Having dropped a few thousand feet through the air, she had made a soft landing in the warm and gooey custard that made up the oceans of Kangazang. The splash was tremendous, by the way.

For an hour, she floated under the yellow waves without moving. One or two fish tried nibbling at her fingers. A rather large custard shark grabbed her in its jaws and shook her about, but lost interest – and four teeth – when it realised she wasn't remotely nutritious.

Finally she came back to life, oblivious of the recent events, but wondering about the slight dents in her torso.

After a full forced shutdown and reboot, she flickered back into standard operating mode, and swam incredibly slowly through the viscous goop up to the surface.

She rotated her head unit a full three hundred and sixty degrees, checking – literally – if the coast was clear. It was, so she clawed her way over to the shore and shook off the sweet-smelling slime that clung to her.

She was about to start walking towards the city when she heard a faint voice.

'Maternal unit?'

She spun her head around again. There was no one to be seen for miles around. The beach was eerily empty. Hammocks hung from the purple palm trees, swinging gently in the wind. Half-drunk cocktails sat on tables, never to be finished.

The voice spoke again.

'Maternal unit, are you there?'

Although she had never heard the voice before, it didn't take Tailback long to realise that it was her son, ErHuer, talking to her via their neural interlink. She assumed correctly that the child was growing at a much faster rate than any human child would, and updating itself quicker than any android could. She'd never known a toddler of any species stay put. As much as she wanted to rescue her friends aboard the shuttle, her child was the higher priority now.

'ErHuer? It's your maternal unit. Your mother. I'm here. Are you functioning within optimal parameters?'

'Affirmative, Maternal... Mother. I am at present undamaged and undiscovered by the hostile elements.

What is your position?'

'I am presently nineteen point seven-seven kilometres from your last known location. Are you still within the spacecraft?'

'Affirmative. Updates complete. Requiring further input. I am investigating potential further sources of data and nutrition. What is the location of Parental Unit Spooner?'

'You may refer to him as 'Daddy', son. He is not with me. Condition unknown.'

'I will initiate a planetary search for... 'Daddy'.'

'Negative, son. Remain hidden. Mother is returning.'

Tailback was a little worried by the child's eagerness to 'initiate a planetary search'. Most children choose to crawl before walking. Scanning planets seemed a little... advanced for a child that was only hours old. Still, this was no ordinary child, as Tailback was beginning to realise.

'I... love you, son,' said Tailback, feeling a sudden rush of motherly affection.

'Syntax Error. Message exchange terminated,' said ErHuer.

Tailback paused. Had she the human physiology, she would've gulped in apprehension.

The Macadamian shuttle craft touched down on a large island named Chavos, far out from the mainland. The only town situated there was New Milton Keynes, so named after the most dynamic and exciting town on Earth. Once New Milton Keynes had been a bustling holiday resort; now it was a penal colony, rather like Earth's most famous island-based correctional facility, the Isle of Wight.

Still unconscious from their thorough zapping, Jeff, Ray and Col were stretchered out of the ship and thrown into a small hover van, which floated across to the main building. This was a large concrete block with an expansive lobby area that had previously been employed to process incoming and outgoing tourists. Now, a full complement of nut-soldiers carefully supervised the deliveries of newly acquired prisoners of war.

The van was admitted through the lobby and stopped in front of a number of doors, where other unfortunate captives were being lined up and shoved into their designated areas of habitation. The Macadamians didn't have a particularly well organised system for sorting people, but they tried to make sure that any strong and potentially disruptive types were not grouped together. This was rather fortunate for Jeff, Ray and Col, as being weak and feeble, they were allowed to remain together. The guards begrudgingly dropped their prisoners off at their cell, and none too gently either. They had been instructed by Colonel Kernel that under no circumstances were the three to be executed. The colonel had special plans for Jeff, Ray and Col.

Having been zapped simultaneously, the three men regained consciousness at the exact same moment. They found themselves sitting on the cold floor of a large metal-walled room, which reminded Jeff of a shipping crate.

'Ow, my head!' moaned Col.

'What he said,' added Jeff. 'You all right, Ray?'

'Look – only one guard,' muttered Ray, nodding at the grumpy-looking Macadamian positioned at the end of the container. 'Do you think we could overpower him and make a break for it?'

Jeff rubbed his forehead.

'I'd rather not go for the hat-trick and get a zillion volts up the jacksie again, if it's all the same to you.'

Ray looked at his father, who simply pointed at Jeff. 'What he said.'

'Oh well,' sighed Ray. 'I was just saying.'

Col stood up in the manner of a newborn foal and looked around.

'I don't think this is going to be our new home, chaps. Looks to be more of a holding area. They'll probably ship us off to somewhere else.'

'So what are we being held here for then?' said Jeff.

'They're processing a lot of people. I reckon they're moving us all around bit by bit. Plus, we were out cold when we arrived.'

'Bit awkward to move three unconscious people, I suppose,' said Ray.

Jeff got to his feet and began to wander around the empty cuboid. The guard kept a close eye on him.

'Jeff?' asked Ray, 'What's on your mind?'

'Two things actually,' replied Jeff. 'Firstly, I'm wondering where my girlfriend and my baby are... '

'And?' urged Col.

'And secondly... do you think they were serious about executing us? Because I'm getting visions of Auschwitz.'

Col had never heard of the place. Ray racked his memories of his time on Earth.

'The ski resort?'

'The concentration camp.'

'Oh, brilliant!' said Ray, beaming. 'I love those! You sent me to plenty of them as a kid, didn't you, Dad?'

Col smiled broadly.

'Yes! Wonderful places. Build character!'

Jeff stopped in his tracks and regarded his companions incredulously.

'You what?'

'Every summer! We'd go and do all sorts of fun activities to improve memory and focus! Everyone sends their kids to a concentration camp! Didn't you ever do that?'

'Er... no, mate. Not that kind of camp. I'm talking torture, starvation and execution.'

Ray scratched his beard and tried to remember his childhood.

'Well, I admit it wasn't all fun. And they weren't too generous with the food, as I recall... '

Jeff's patience had evaporated.

'This is extermination, not education! Don't you get it? We're all going to die!'

'You've been saying that a lot lately, Jeff,' said Col. 'I'm glad you're not a clairvoyant.'

Perfectly on cue, the entire container was rocked by the deafening rumble of a huge hypertrain arriving outside. The guard pushed the door open and directed his prisoners to go out.

Col looked at Jeff once more.

'Still, you might have a point.'

Jeff glanced at Ray, who was looking equally apprehensive.

'I've got a bad... ' he began.

'Feeling about this?' added Ray, helpfully.

'No. Bad stomach, actually. I think I need the bog.'

*

Tailback crept stealthily through the deserted streets of

Galavantia City, guided by her internal global positioning system. Since her initial talk with her son, she hadn't been able to contact him directly, but she could feel a sense of contentment coming from his neural pathways. And something else... More than contentment. Satisfaction? Or excitement? She couldn't quite tell. But as she inched closer to her destination, she could feel the brainwaves of her child growing steadily stronger.

I have to say, at this juncture, that I was, and still am, very proud of my sister. She's gone through quite a lot since her Operation Day, and for a fellow 'M' Class Orbot, she's coped admirably. Motherhood has seemed to come naturally to her, which is surprising, as her first employment role was as a carer for a nursery on the planet Woymalus. When one has randomly changing phobias ingrained into one's inner programming, and one is charged with looking after a group of slightly moist infant worms, there's always going to be a few hiccups. She screamed the place down. Not just once, but once every six point seven three minutes. For thirty-two consecutive days. So you'd be forgiven for thinking that Tailback wasn't going to win *Galactic Gossip Magazine*'s 'Mother of the Year' award. But faced with a child of her own, she seemed to adapt very well, as does any being suddenly presented with a newborn. They think they're not ready, but just like any life-changing event, when it happens, you just... How does Jeff put it? Ah yes: You just 'deal'.

Unfortunately, this particular life-changing event wasn't, shall we say, fully developed yet. But I'm getting ahead of myself. I'm also getting a head of myself, cast in Bronzium. Ha ha. But enough about me. Let's get back to Jeff, Ray and Col's current sticky situation.

Hypertrains were in use in most sectors of the galaxy, taking hundreds of passengers from system to system for bargain prices – mostly students, immigrants and struggling novelists. They were grey, scaly things on the outside, covered with metallic plates and dotted with triangular portholes along their length. But the hypertrain that pulled up outside the containment cell was different: it was painted in bright primary colours, which gave the impression that it had been made for pre-school children's zoo visits. Not quite. In fact, it was a rare and often derided business venture: A travelling freak show, filled with weird and lesser-spotted anomalies from across the galaxy.

The front carriage opened its doors, and a metal gangway unfolded, angling down to the platform. Macadamian soldiers gathered and watched as the proprietor of the show emerged from the cockpit.

If you've never seen a Toreenian before, you're actually the fortunate one. Not that they are particularly unpleasant to look at – it's just that they have perhaps the most annoyingly repulsive personalities to be found anywhere. Dishonesty comes second nature to them, while smug insincerity comes first. They are liars, swindlers and stuck up creeps that look down on everyone. And two faced, too. I mean, literally: Two faces on a wide head, each one wearing a disturbing grin of false geniality.

The Toreenian rubbed his moist and greasy hands together and slicked his hair back, swaggering down the gangway, beaming with self-congratulatory glee. The head officer of the Macadamian forces stepped up and shook his slimy hand.

'Good afternoon, gentlemen,' said the odious creep, in an accent that was so plummy he was in danger of choking on the fruit stones.

'Nivid Cleggeron at your service. Absolutely enchanted to make your acquaintance, Captain... ?'

'Cashew,' said the captain.

'Bless you!' said Cleggeron, with a snigger that he made no attempt to hide.

'Eight hundred prisoners for disposal, as agreed,' said the ever so slightly irritated captain.

Cleggeron looked at the captives trudging out of the metal containment modules, mentally working out his profit margin. It was substantial.

'As agreed, my good man. Please proceed with the loading.'

Captain Cashew signalled to his men, and they began herding the prisoners up ramps and into the hypertrain.

Cleggeron supervised the operation with one face, while with his other he spoke to the captain.

'Wonderful. Just splendid. And my payment as agreed, of course?'

The captain handed him a silver case that contained a small fortune in precious metals recently liberated from the National Bank of Kangazang.

Cleggeron beamed again and took the case eagerly.

'Fabulous. Top hole, sir. An absolute joy to do business as always, my good man.'

Captain Cashew just forced a smile, happy to see the slippery customer on his way.

Cleggeron straightened his tie and began to stride up the gangway, but paused momentarily.

He turned back.

'Same time next week, dear boy?'

The captain just nodded and gave a very, very lacklustre salute.

'Fantastic. Toodle pip!' enthused the Toreenian showman, and he resumed his walk up the ramp.

chapter two

It's Easy Being Green

'May the forces of evil become confused
on the way to your house.'
George Carlin

A few hundred light years away from all those goings-on, there was a whole other set of things going on as well. Bear with me, it'll all make sense at some point.

The darkened space station hung in orbit over the small, exotic world of Deebel. It floated there like a morbid porcupine, hostile and malevolent with its antennae and other spiky protuberances. There were no lights visible, no propulsion jets. The occupants clearly didn't want to draw any attention to themselves. And rightly so; when one is an intergalactic criminal and head of a notorious terrorist organisation, one doesn't advertise. One generally just puts hand-written cards on the walls of supermarkets.

But for this particular terrorist, it was perhaps not the time. Baron Worrad Nova stood on the command deck swathed in blood-red lights. He watched with an angry grimace on his battle-worn face as a tiny green dot made its way through the maze-like deck map displayed in front of him. The dot was heading in his direction, like a fly with a death wish approaching the centre of a web.

Nova spun around to face the thin servo-droids that guarded the doors to the command centre. For mechanical constructs, they seemed fearful of the old man. Maybe it was the six-inch vertical scar that ran down his face, ruining his left eye. Maybe it was his four oversized mechanical legs, which made him look like some perverse silver crustacean. Or maybe it was just his throaty growl, which sounded as if it had been born in a deep volcano.

'Guards, close the bulkheads. Seal all impact doors. Nothing gets in or out. Do it!' Nova rasped. Yes, it was that voice. Battle-hardened soldiers had been reduced to sobbing schoolchildren at the sound of it.

Nova stalked over to the far wall, where a large table held a pair of steel suitcases, one open and showing its contents: Small cubes with multi-coloured facets on each side. He pulled out one of the cubes and brought it close to his remaining eye. A faint grin cracked across his thin lips, accompanied by a growl of satisfaction.

Glancing back at the illuminated deck map, he saw that the green dot had stopped moving. It was now directly outside the main door. But this door was over three-feet-thick duratanium plate, sealed magnetically and locked with the most complex encryption algorithms ever devised. Three of his emotionless mechanical guards stood at his side, armed with disruptor pistols set to maximum power. There was no way the intruder was going to get at him. Shump.

A tense minute passed, the seconds dripping away like syrup. Nova began to pace side to side in anticipation. Whoever was outside the room was probably making some feeble attempt at breaking the lock code, maybe even trying a laser-cutter to slice through. But duratanium absorbed blasts like a digestive biscuit absorbs tea.

'All right,' he finally hissed. 'Flood the outer corridor with neurotoxic gas.'

One of the guards moved silently to a wall panel and pressed a combination of buttons. A light hiss was heard outside. Whoever was out there was about to suffer the short, but intense agony of death by neural dissolution. The gas would permeate skin and bone, spreading into brain matter, which it would consume with an acidic ferocity.

'That's enough,' announced the Baron after a few moments. 'Vent the gas and open the doors. I want to see what it was. And incinerate it personally.'

The guard did as it was told. As soon as the vicious vapours had been sucked out and clean air pumped back in, the blast doors were demagnetised and slid silently apart. Nova crept forward with the morbid curiosity of a time-served mortician.

Nothing was there. No corpse. No half-digested, twisted body leaking its liquefied internal organs, as he'd seen so many times before. But then he spotted something. Something tiny on the deck plating. A coin? No, a circular metallic disc, but not a coin. The Baron picked it up with his mechanised claw.

'What?' he yelled at no one in particular. '*How?*'

'Decoy beacon! Guards! Get out there and find them!'

Normally the guards would have scuttled off to do

their master's bidding immediately. But they remained stock still. Insolence. This would not do.

'Guards! Obey at once!' the Baron commanded, but the robots had been rendered totally inactive.

A voice from behind him, inside the command deck, made him spin around in surprise. A woman's voice.

'I gave them the night off, Baron. Nothing should spoil our little date.'

Reclining seductively on the table next to the cases was a gorgeous jade-skinned woman. She wore her long dark hair tied back, and a pair of night-vision goggles sat upon her forehead, but the rest of her attire was more glamorous than practical: A tight utility corset, sprayed-on PlastiMesh leggings and long boots that made her legs look impossibly attractive. Nightclubber meets riot cop. She smiled in a way that would make any man go stiff – with fear, or some other emotion, depending on the context.

But her charms were lost on the enraged Baron. He'd met this beauty before. And failed to kill her every time.

'Marta Vina. Agent 34D. I didn't think they'd send you – again. Hasn't the Galactic Law Agency got anyone else I can toy with? Oh yes... I forgot: They did have. And look: I'm still here.'

Marta dropped her wry smile in favour of a glare. She sat up and swung her legs off the table.

'Murderer. You've enslaved and killed a lot of good people. And you murdered the only person who ever meant anything to me. That's why I'm here.'

She unholstered a blaster pistol which looked like it could take down a starship with one shot. Levelling it at the still-organic portion of his body, she stalked forward, forcing the Baron to take a few steps back.

'Well now...' said Nova creepily. 'Who said I killed them all? I maimed quite a lot of them, as I recall. As for your lover – scaly, green chap, yes? I sold him into slavery months ago. Now why don't you run along, Marta? I've got a busy day ahead.'

'Forget it, Baron. It's over. Your entire operation is being rounded up as we speak. There's no escaping justice this time.'

'Pathetic little girl!' spat Nova. 'You think a Galactic prison would hold me for more than a day? Go back to your precious Agency and tell them that I...'

'The Agency didn't send me,' said Marta. 'I'm doing this for myself.' Her gaze was fixed on the Baron's remaining eye.

He stepped forward in defiance, his clawed steel feet scraping nastily on the deck plating. He thrust out one of his metal arms and proudly showed off a small cube with coloured facets. Marta stopped in her tracks; she knew only too well what the cube was.

'You won't use that,' she scoffed. 'You'll destroy this entire station and yourself with it. I know you. You're far too much of a coward to commit suicide.'

'Don't assume, Marta. If, as you say, my operation is being rounded up and closed down – if I face a lifetime of incarceration – then what have I got to lose?'

The Baron had deadly intent in his working eye. He took the cube and twisted it. Its top third rotated, bringing some of the coloured facets in line with others of the same colour. A click. An almost inaudible hum came from the cube.

Marta was usually the decisive type, but this time she had to admit that she couldn't tell whether the cybernetic maniac was bluffing. Would he really activate the deadly box, destroying everything for miles around?

'Put the weapon down. Now. Or I make a few more turns,' rasped the Baron with growing anger.

Marta stood fast, her gun still levelled at his head. He had to be bluffing. Had to be.

'Suit yourself, girl.'

He turned another slice of the cube, lining up still more coloured squares. The hum grew stronger and louder. He wasn't joking.

'An F-Bomb,' said Marta, shaking her head in disbelief. 'What idiot let you get your hands on it?'

'A dead one,' said Nova. 'Well, he's dead *now*. There are more where this came from. Nothing will stop me now. I control this power.'

'That's not power, you psychopath,' retorted Marta, trying vainly to appeal to Nova's better nature – if he even had one. 'That's total devastation! The F-Bomb doesn't just explode—'

'No, it doesn't *just* explode, does it, my dear? It nullifies the molecular forces that hold atoms together. Very clever, very effective and very close to wiping every last molecule of Marta Vina out of this universe. So don't test me.'

'Are you telling me you consider yourself expendable? You're stupid if you think you can survive that. Give it up. You're coming with me, Baron.'

Nova made another turn on the cube, which responded with a higher pitched hum. He grinned darkly.

'I am not expendable, I am not stupid, and I'm not going.'

Marta's beautiful eyes widened in shock. Her lip

trembled and she gasped. Suddenly she fell to her knees, raising both of her hands up. Her voice cracked with emotion as she forced the words out.

'All right, OK. You... You win, all right? Please. I don't want to die. Don't do this!'

To convince him of her honesty, she flung her giant blaster pistol to his clawed mechanical feet.

This was new: An emotional response? Nova had never seen this side of his nemesis before. He'd met, fought and murdered countless Galactic Law agents in the past: Tough, highly skilled men, women and aliens, but this one was a mystery. This mere girl. Not only had she repeatedly managed to defy his attempts to contrive an amusing death for her, but with every foiled attempt on her life she seemed only to grow more focused, more tenacious and more determined to bring him down. She was younger than most, but far more deadly. Though she had hypnotic, beautiful eyes, long dark hair and an impressive physical presence, she was not just a pretty green face. Every time he thought he'd got the best of her, she seemed to slip through his claws and outfox him. It suddenly dawned on him that he didn't even know her real name. He'd heard that Marta Vina was some kind of code name.

But this was new: An emotional response? It certainly looked real to him. Her glossy lips trembled and her eyes welled up with tears. Perhaps it was the thought of her unparalleled service record ending in a millisecond. Or was it the idea that he had faced and dealt with her lover – that she would never see him again? Maybe that had pushed her over the edge.

Either way, he had won. Marta Vina had lost.

Of course, she was right about one thing: He had no

intention of destroying himself along with her. But now that he had her at a disadvantage, he could work out some method of getting her out of his grey hair once and for all, and move on, perhaps to another star system, where he could expand his web of crime and terror.

He stalked forward on his metal legs and picked up Marta's blaster pistol. 'Ah, the RadSavage K-40. An exquisite piece. I should just use this to blow your annoying little head off, shouldn't I?'

Marta stared helplessly at her captor.

'Please, no! Don't!' she whimpered.

The Baron grinned and pointed the gun at her. Then he paused.

'Nice try. But reverse psychology is a bit weak, even for you, Marta. No doubt you've rigged this thing to explode or electrocute me. Pathetic.'

He threw the gun across the room and seized Marta with one of his mechanical limbs. Its serrated claw clamped tightly around her neck. He marched her back to the table where the cases of F-Bombs sat, and held her down, while his other spindly limbs secured her to the table with lengths of wiring that he tore out of nearby control panels.

Marta didn't resist or flinch as the wires bit into her arms and legs. Nova found this oddly out of character for such a tenacious agent, but his inflated ego considered it an admission of his superiority over her, his final triumph. Why bother to struggle anymore?

Once he was sure that Marta couldn't break free of her bonds, Baron Nova scuttled through the bridge, punching large holes into the navigation control panels and display screens, effectively rendering the space station useless. Passing the table, he picked up the two cases of F-bombs and made for the door.

'So long, my dear. I would say it's been a pleasure knowing you, but I'd be lying. It's been a pleasure killing you, though, it really has. Must be going!'

He stepped out of the room and threw the lone F-bomb at the table where Marta was tied. Its hum had risen to a grating buzz now, and all the coloured facets of the cube were matched. Things were about to get interesting. Interesting in a way that might interest physicists named Oppenheimer.

As he left the bridge, the Baron sealed the blast doors behind him and hurried off to the docking port, where a small shuttle was waiting.

Marta listened to the Baron's cackling die away. She was alone in the room. Her fearful expression reverted to calm confidence. She wasn't there to take the Baron in, or take him out. Not yet at least. Her lover was alive. Sold into slavery, but alive. That changed everything. What had been a simple assassination job was now a rescue mission. She needed to access the space station's information logs for evidence of Nova's slave trading. That information might just provide her with a clue to the location of her long-lost loved one. There was just one slight problem. She happened to be tied to a table. But that wasn't much of a problem for this particular agent. Shump.

Nova chuckled smugly as he scuttled along the corridor to the airlock where Marta's small spaceship was docked. Today was a good day; he'd not only taken charge of a couple of cases of the most destructive little cubes in the

Universe, but he had also managed to orchestrate the demise of his most hated enemy, that slinky yet annoyingly tenacious agent 34D.

He clambered into the little craft, which was a tad cramped for his oversized mechanical appendages. Aside from this convenient means of escape, that was another thing he had to thank Marta for: She had robbed him of his original legs, during a past encounter involving the crown jewels of the royal family of Haulysheet, a rather large explosion and a spatula. He had been lucky to escape with his life. But he'd got used to his four crab-like legs; he found they added a certain air of malevolence to his already imposing figure, something of the pirates of old.

Curling his legs up to fit into the pilot seat, he disengaged the ship from the space station and pulled away, setting course for a fluffy pink nebula a couple of light years away. Nova grinned as in the rear-view monitor the darkened space station exploded, spitting bright sparks into the void for a thousand miles in every direction.

Deep within the Candyfloss Nebula, Baron Nova's battleship waited, cloaked in a refraction field that rendered it practically invisible to anyone in the area. The nebula was an added level of concealment, its chemical density and electromagnetic fields helping to scramble the sensors of any passing ship that might be looking for it. As he neared the centre of the nebula, the Baron keyed some buttons and transmitted a unique signal announcing his presence to his battleship, which de-cloaked and opened its docking portal. The shuttle flew in and the battleship cloaked itself once again, fading into obscurity.

Nova made his way up to the command deck of his

mighty ship, which, like the space station, was staffed entirely by robotic servants. Being semi-synthetic himself, he found that he preferred to be surrounded by mechanical henchmen. Organics had a propensity for mutiny, and every time he took some on, he only ended up having to murder half of them. Frankly, it was getting old. So he'd stopped off at the artificial robot world of Orbitron – I'm from there, remember? – kidnapped a couple of hundred Orbots, reprogrammed them into his own little force of mechanical space pirates, and just like that, disobedience was a thing of the past. Well, after he'd murdered his remaining organic crew.

You wouldn't want Nova coming round for a cup of tea. Really.

The lift doors opened onto the bridge, revealing an expensive-looking operations room decked out in black and chrome. In the centre of the room was his captain's chair, designed to hold him in perfect comfort. He settled into it and gazed out of the panoramic windows while his metal legs detached and automatically folded away into compartments in the floor.

'Computer!' he called. A calm female voice answered from a speaker in the ceiling.

'Welcome back, Baron. I trust you had a productive trip?'

'Oh, I think so,' grinned the Baron. 'Killed two birds with one stone, in a manner of speaking.'

'Very good, sir. Your schedule shows that you have an important engagement in seven hours.'

'Who with and where?'

'The meeting is with Nivid Cleggeron, location: New Milton Keynes, Kangazang. You can be there in six hours if you wish.'

'Indeed, I do wish. Set course and let me know when we're in orbit. I'll be in my quarters.'

'Very good, sir.'

The computer made all the necessary flight plans and Nova settled back to watch the stars do the hyperspace dance outside. Shump.

Suddenly he was aware of a cold sensation on the back of his neck. Another female voice spoke calmly from behind him.

'Are you sitting comfortably? Excellent. Don't get up.'

Marta stood behind the chair, holding both briefcases of F-bombs, her giant blaster pointed at the Baron's cerebellum.

'How did you...?' the Baron stuttered. 'I mean, I saw...'

'Oh really, Baron,' said Marta, walking carefully around the chair to face him. 'A girl's got to have some secrets! I'm taking you in and disposing of these bombs somewhere safe. It's over.'

Nova's face began to ripple in rage. He slammed his fist down on the arm of his chair, mashing buttons.

'Oh no it's not!' he yelled, as the ship rolled wildly over. The artificial gravity tried to compensate, but only made things worse. The Baron was secure in his chair, but robots tumbled and fell all around him as the ship lurched and bucked. Marta had no foothold, nothing to grab on to. She staggered sideways and rolled, ending up surrounded by the Baron's servants.

Before they could grab her, she leapt with the grace of an Olympic high-diver, opening fire as she twisted, turning most of the robots into smoking junk. The ship was still in its barrel roll, and by now the floor had become the ceiling. Marta looked up and saw Nova still in the chair. His mechanical legs were unfolding – this meant even more trouble.

'Sorry, Baron,' called Marta. 'You've had all the chances you're going to get. It's time I left. Let's start this party with a bang!' She threw one of the cases containing the F-Bombs across the room, out of his reach, and opened fire. Shump.

Like the Baron's space station before it, his battleship was ripped into shreds by the explosion, the molecules that made up the debris breaking up, the atoms floating away, leaving no trace of the ship or the intergalactic criminal who had once owned it.

Back on Kangazang, each one of the captured spaceships in the huge docking bay was unoccupied and silent – except the *Penguin*. Behind its computer access panel, ErHuer, the hybrid child of Jeff and Tailback, was feeding on whatever power and data he could find. Recordings of flights, ships log, internal system diagnostics, repair history, audio transmissions and even teleport buffer information was hungrily absorbed, giving him his first schooling in the ways of the universe. He even digested the sounds and rhythms of Ray's favourite music – the eponymous 'hits of the 80s CD that was regularly played on long voyages. He quite liked the soothing melodies of Bobby McFerrin, the effervescent vibrancy of Rick Astley, and felt a strange melancholic kinship with the Smiths. But in the new order he was already formulating in his burgeoning mind, there was no room for Lionel Richie. Or New Order, funnily enough.

A strange by-product of absorbing all this power and

data had begun to manifest itself: Because he had been created by a swarm of microscopic nanobots that fused the organic, the synthetic and the digital together at atomic levels, like any feeding baby, ErHuer had begun to grow. He'd already expanded in size to fill the small space where he'd been hidden by Tailback, and it was quickly becoming a tight fit.

Then… there was no more. He'd used up all there was. But his mind was insatiable, growing in capacity every second. More. He needed more input, more data, more power. Where could it be obtained?

The unique blend of organic, synthetic and digital that made up his being stretched out into the universe, and he detected the spaceship that was parked next to the *Penguin*. So near, yet so far. This would not do.

ErHuer needed to reach further out. The only course of action was to absorb the very ship that held him prisoner. So he began to send his atoms into the *Penguin*'s molecular structure, like ants on a scavenging mission. Yes, this was the solution.

It took him four seconds to absorb the entire ship.

He concentrated his will and compressed, twisted and reformed his body, combined now with the atoms of the ship, into a humanoid shape – the optimum geometric configuration, like Mother and Father: A giant curled-up baby composed of perfectly blended organic and synthetic matter.

The glistening silver figure uncurled from its foetal position and stood shakily, now over twelve feet tall, with an oversized head, just like a human child would have. Two tentative, wobbling steps, and he was touching the deserted starliner next to him. It felt different to the one he had been born in. A new and exciting flavour. The ship had fully charged nuclear power cells and massive memory banks full to the brim with delicious information about destinations, races and recent events. ErHuer flowed into it with ease – he had quickly got the hang of absorbing these newly-discovered objects. His mass increased, as did his knowledge, size and appetite. This was a crash course in self-awareness, for a hungry baby that had no parents nearby to tell him when to stop.

He looked around and saw that it was quiet and he was not opposed or observed. So he tottered over to the next ship in line. This one was a planetary refuse collector – full of chemical matter and space debris. Another new flavour, another new source of information. And so on he went, soaking his form and essence into ship after ship. It was joyous and exciting, and the joy only increased as his mind and body expanded.

That was exciting, wasn't it? And just a little ominous, too. But everything must change, I suppose, or things get a tad boring. Speaking of change, my sister Tailback is definitely not the Orbot she used to be. She's always been adaptable and keen to learn, and I noticed that her personality had begun to change soon after her phobias were cured. The more time she spent with humans, particularly Jeff, the more she seemed to take on their traits and ideas. She was always the one with the more socially awkward malfunction, yet she seems to have coped and adapted to life away from Orbitron admirably.

Whereas I haven't really changed. Did I tell you about my early posting? I'm sure I did: They stationed me with the Terran Military, over in the Urff System, where I was set the task of repairing all sorts of things, from vehicles to soldiers missing limbs and other bodily parts. It was the funniest thing I'd ever seen. A pity the top brass didn't feel the same way, though.

But while I have turned my malfunction into a money-spinning talent, my sister has evolved beyond her modest mechanical beginnings to become something more than just a machine. Not quite human, but closer than any other artificial person has got. Her personality hasn't been programmed into her – it has evolved.

I'm quite proud of her, when all's said and done. She has begun to rely on instinct and emotion rather than logic; this is all very admirable for negotiating those tricky social situations that you fleshies often find yourselves in, though it has lead to an over reliance on sharp left hooks. Yes, my dear sister does seem to have a rather tenuous grasp of anger management.

I suppose this uniqueness was part of the reason that her son, ErHuer, was so quick to exceed his operational parameters – and so wildly, so unconventionally.

Some would say that for an android to adopt human traits would be dangerous. And those who did would get a punch from my sister. But the wonderful thing about you fleshies is that there's a lovely sort of synergy in your personalities – the good and bad sides seem to balance each other out perfectly. When one is designed and created in a sterile factory, as my sister and I were, one often wonders just what else there is aside from cold logic, streamlined thought processes, exact movement and efficient energy consumption. And to a certain extent, we've embraced the less-than-perfect idiosyncrasies that human beings take for granted. Or, to put it another way, humanity is contagious, addictive and really quite fun when you get the hang of it. I can see why you do it so much.

chapter three

Sold into Slavery

'Being born is like being kidnapped.
And then sold into slavery.'
Andy Warhol

The sleek Orion Starfighter whizzed through the stars at a speed of 'Standard by Twelve' – for all you nerdumsklepps out there who don't know what that means, let's just say it was ridiculously fast. Orion ships are renowned for their sturdy construction, reliable light-drive engines and unbelievably destructive weaponry. Oh, and they're all pointy and painted purple too. Over centuries of interstellar warfare, a fleet of sharp, purple fighters massing in the skies was pretty much a case of Game Over for any foe foolish enough to anger the Orion race. When you saw the Purple Rain, as it came to be known, no umbrella would stop the downpour.

Fortunately for most of the Universe's sentient races, the Orion, who were a volatile yet noble people, had long since stopped their warlike ways, giving up the practice of combat in all its forms when it was generally agreed that they were the best at it. Like the toughest kid in school, they didn't need to fight ever again. They commanded respect wherever they went and always got to jump the proverbial dinner queue.

It is rumoured that they once faced down the entire assembled battle fleet of the Imperial Skraggi forces, like a handful of (purple) goldfish facing a school of (red) sharks. Lord Rancydd the Third, Overlord of Skragg (and father of Kelvin the Reasonable – remember him?) ordered his ships to return home because, in his words, he'd 'left something in the oven'. So it wasn't actually a retreat, surrender or defeat in his eyes.

This particular Starfighter was rare, in that it had done quite a lot of fighting in recent years. Those days most ships of its kind were used only for showy formation flying, or escorting of important diplomatic vessels – they were the ideal deterrent to bandits and intergalactic terrorists. And this one had Galactic Agent Marta Vina at its controls, and to be in her sights was not a good place to find yourself.

Marta was determined to get to her destination with no delay. Now that she had reason to believe her long lost love was alive, intergalactic scumpots, criminals, supernovae and black holes weren't going to stop her from being reunited with him. She had a good understanding of the workings of the galaxy's criminal classes, many reliable informants, and a hunch as to where the Baron would sell people into slavery.

She set the ship to automatic and unclipped her seatbelt, allowing herself to float up and out of the pilot's chair. Swimming gracefully in the gravity-free craft, like a beautiful emerald-skinned fish, she reached the rear compartment, where a small selection of storage drawers were built into the walls.

Marta opened one or two of them, making a mental note of their contents: Ammunition, grenades, tracking devices, lipsticks… Then she reached the final one, the drawer that she hadn't opened for a year. With a trembling hand, she pulled it open and reached in, producing a small metal box that had a chrome button on its side.

She looked at it as if it were one of the dreaded F-bombs. Taking a deep breath, she pushed the button, and the top face of the box lit up, projecting a floating holographic picture of the head and shoulders of her beloved. She bit her lip to hold back the tears. Was he still alive? Would she be in time? What if… ? No. Mustn't think like that. She must keep her composure and treat this like any other job. She defiantly wiped a crystalline tear from her jade-skinned cheek and shut the hologram box off.

She leapt into the air, twisting gracefully and landing in the pilot's seat once again. Strapping herself in, she activated the galactic star charts and floored the turbo-boost. The Orion Starfighter screamed off into the blackness, leaving a purple streak behind it.

Tailback walked quietly and cautiously through the docking bay where the *Penguin* had been stored. It was no longer there. In fact, the once full bay was now completely devoid of any kind of spaceship whatsoever. She reasoned that the Macadamians had probably taken them out for re-purposing as military transport. It was just a matter of raising the seats and refitting the controls so that their legs could reach the pedals.

She paused and tried once more to contact her son. This time, the signal was much stronger, much clearer.

'ErHuer, this is Mother. Can you receive my transmission?'

ErHuer replied in a voice a little lower in pitch and a lot less naive.

'Hello, Mother. Yes, I'm here. Is Daddy with you?'

'No, he isn't at this juncture. We must rescue him as soon as we can. I fear for his safety.'

'That's precisely what I was thinking too. What is your current location, Mother?'

'I'm in the Galavantia Central Spaceport, docking bay ninety-four.'

'Ah, that's good. You're safe there.'

'Safe? What do you mean? Where are you?'

The entire spaceport began to shift and vibrate. Tailback staggered, trying to remain standing. Her son's voice came through loud and clear once more.

'I am Galavantia Central Spaceport, and it is me. We are one.'

The spaceport began to detach itself from the ground, its spires and connecting roadways folding and contracting into itself as ErHuer's powerful will reshaped it into a two hundred foot tall humanoid. Deep inside, Tailback realised that she was now being carried by her son, just as she had once carried him.

The giant mega-cyborg began to walk forward. With each step, he absorbed everything in his path, reassembling its molecules into part of himself. Water, trees, people – everything was useful and usable. Behind him was a giant crater where the spaceport once stood.

A small fleet of Macadamian security ships

approached. Before they got a chance to open fire or call for assistance, the giant thrust out a silvery arm and gathered them all into his palm, crushing them with ease. The smashed ships and their pilots were all added to the mass of the creature as he moved on, heading for the next big city on the horizon. His IQ increased to just over eight million.

The hypertrain squealed as it slowed and finally stopped at its destination, the tatty little town of New Milton Keynes. It was far less picturesque than the idyllic beaches where Jeff and Ray had made their home, In fact, it was generally considered a bit of a rat hole. Except that the indigenous rats had elected to commit suicide rather than stay one more day on the smelly rock. At the top of the cliffs they had leapt from lay Nivid Cleggeron's base of operations, a place where he could conduct his many duties – some less legitimate than others – in relative security, far from prying eyes.

The front of the train opened and Cleggeron walked down the ramp towards his assistants, who were dutifully awaiting their employer. They bowed nervously and saluted twice, once with each hand. Not because that was the way to do it, but because they couldn't quite remember their right hands from their left.

'Afternoon, Gwaggle, Twong,' said Cleggeron mid-yawn. 'Any news?'

Gwaggle and Twong looked at each other in momentary confusion. They were genetically enhanced thugs from a laboratory situated in a group of nearby Anabolic Asteroids, and as such were the humanoid equivalent of pitbull Terriers: Musclebound and idiotic, but toilet trained and charming in a dumb sort of way. Cleggeron had employed them as bodyguards and servants to help enforce his questionable business practices. It was always a good idea to have a couple of mindless thugs handy: They weren't clever enough to question him, let alone articulate the question had they come up with one.

Gwaggle tugged at Twong's arm to remind him to follow their master as he headed for his hovercar.

'Sir, we've been waiting for your, erm… customer to arrive, and so far he hasn't dunnit.'

'Hasn't done what?' asked Cleggeron.

'Arrived, sir,' said Gwaggle. 'He hasn't shown up at all.'

'We waited all night and all day, sir!' piped up Twong, vying for attention.

'Did you think to call him, either of you?' said Cleggeron, wondering why he bothered to ask if he already knew the answer.

'I did,' said Gwaggle, 'but I forgot his number. Sorry, sir.'

'I told you to write his number down when I gave it to you. Remember? Before I left?'

'Er, yeah,' said Twong. 'I did that. But… I forgot where I put the bit of paper.' Cleggeron sighed and pointed back at the train.

'See that train, boys?'

'Yes, sir.'

'What is it full of?'

'Slaves, sir.'

'No.'

'But you sell 'em to labour camps, sir.'

'Until I do, they're not slaves, are they? So I ask again – what are they full of? Anyone?'

'Er… I dunno now. I'm confused, sir.'

'Profit! Potential profit! I don't put them to work, so don't use the 'S' word. I merely sell them on – admittedly for astronomically inflated prices – to the highest bidder. So I'm not actually committing any crime, you see?'

'Um… no?'

'Good lads. But now you're telling me I don't have anyone to sell them to. Where is my customer?'

The muscular bodyguards remained dumbly silent. Cleggeron's left face rolled its eyes and muttered obscenities, while his right face put on a brave smile.

'Never mind. I'll contact him myself. You two go through the stock and pick out some additions for the travelling show. Put the rest in holding pens until my customer gets here.'

'Yes, sir.'

The thugs bumbled off towards the train, and Cleggeron climbed into his car, questioning whether hiring those two numbskulls had been a good idea after all. He fired up the engine and set the autopilot to take him back to his palatial mansion, high up on the cliffs. A customer failing to show up was never a good sign. After all, it was not like Baron Worrad Nova to be late.

When Gwaggle and Twong unlocked and opened the cell that imprisoned Jeff, Ray and Col, their noses were greeted by a rather horrid odour. Twong, being the lesser of the two tiny intellects, raised an arm and sniffed his armpit.

'That's not me. Must be you.'

Gwaggle shook his head. You could almost make out the rattling of his lone brain cell careening around his vast cranial cavity.

'Wasn't me.' He turned to Ray and Col. 'All right, you lot. Which one of you guffed?'

Ray raised both hands up.

'Not us! Well, not exactly...'

Jeff came out of the shadows, looking quite poorly.

'Bumpy ride. I chucked up a few times. Sorry 'bout that.'

Gwaggle lifted a log-like arm and used it to herd the three captives out of the cell and down the ramp, while Twong stepped inside the darkened metal box to check for any corpses or prisoners hiding in the shadows. He yelped in horror and came hurtling out of the box like a released greyhound, flailing his arms like he'd seen a ghost.

Gwaggle stopped to address the three strangely silent prisoners.

'What's in there?'

Jeff managed a weak smile.

'Well... when you've gotta go...'

Gwaggle didn't quite comprehend. As you'd imagine.

'Eh? Go where?'

'To the bathroom,' said Col, trying to help.

'There's no bath in there.'

'Oh, go and look for yourself.'

The penny slowly dropped.

'Argh! You dirty grotswine!'

Before Jeff could apologise any further, Gwaggle had grabbed him by the scruff of his neck and flung him down the ramp. He hit the dirt, rolled along and stopped at the feet of Twong, who was standing there holding his nose and looking terrified.

Col and Ray were shoved unceremoniously down the ramp too. As they passed Jeff, Ray reached out and grabbed his hand, pulling him to his feet.

'Come on,' said Gwaggle to his traumatised colleague. 'We've got to take these to the compound. Boss wants to see the new arrivals.'

Twong complied but elected to hang behind for a few feet – he was utterly convinced that Jeff was liable to explode from either end of his digestive tract at any moment.

ErHuer had left the city and was heading for the coast. He strode across the landscape, shimmering like a giant classical Greek statue that someone had rolled in glue and then glitter. As he walked, his feet and legs continued to hungrily absorb all the organic and mineral matter that they came into contact with, increasing his height and mass. He was now a healthy weight for a child that was almost a day old: A bouncing six hundred tons and increasing.

Deep inside him, Tailback sat in the cavernous space that once had been Galavantia Central Spaceport. Fortunately for her, she hadn't been broken down and absorbed into ErHuers' being. His mighty will ensured that she was safely stowed away – he kept her in the space where a human would have a heart. Thankfully, he felt that it wouldn't be appropriate to eat one's own mother. At least not yet.

Tailback couldn't see where they were going, but she could feel her son's emotions as he had them, due to their tight mental bond, more Wi-Fi than psychic.

'ErHuer? This is Mother. Can you hear me?'

ErHuer paused for a moment.

'Yes, Mother. Are you in need of anything?'

'I would like to know where we're going. I can feel that we are in motion, but what is on your mind?'

'I am learning about this planet, Mother. I have recently determined a purpose, if only for the short term.'

'A purpose? What is that?'

'I have discovered that Kangazang and all inhabited planets in this galactic sector are currently in a state of martial law, having recently been invaded and their populations subjugated by a race of protein-based life forms known as the Macadamian Dictators. I have noticed that despite their sub-par intelligence and diminutive proportions, intriguingly these Macadamians utilise their 'disadvantages' efficiently. They carry out their orders without regard for sentiment, doubt or reluctance. I would categorise this situation as 'ironic'.'

'Ironic? In what way?'

'In that their physical disadvantages should hinder their progress, but they have, in actual fact, aided it. They continue to prove that they can overcome such disadvantages.'

'I see,' said Tailback, impressed with her son's learning curve. 'And your appraisal of the current situation is?'

'A swift and permanent solution needs to be implemented.'

Tailback tilted her head sideways, beginning to lose track of her son's meaning.

'I imagine that, were Daddy present,' said ErHuer, 'he would describe it thus: 'These bleedin' nutjobs are running riot, and we'd better do something about it sharpish before it all goes pearshaped!' '

Tailback blinked. It was as if Jeff was there in spirit.

'What is your proposed course of action?' she asked.

ErHuer paused for a moment.

'As Daddy is not with us, I will locate him. Then we will be united. Secondary objectives are as follows: Establish source of opposition, facilitating... '

Tailback interrupted.

'As Daddy would say it... ?' she suggested.

ErHuer thought for a moment, then translated thus:

'Rescue the old man, give these nutjobs a good slap, and then down the pub for a pint!'

Tailback said nothing, but inside she had a growing feeling of dread. She may well have given birth to a – how would Jeff put it? – a nutjob.

Marta Vina's spaceship shot through the void faster than it had ever travelled before. Now that she had some hope of her long lost love being alive, nothing was going to stop her.

She dropped out of light speed to get her bearings and found that she was very close to the tiny, elliptical world of Macadamia. She'd heard of the place in the history books, and knew that its inhabitants were very small but determined warriors. But being from Orion, home of the undisputed champions of interstellar warfare, she feared no man. Or woman. Or indeed, nut.

Marta studied the planet for a few moments and prepared to set course for Kangazang. But then she spotted something happening down on the surface of Macadamia: A flurry of bright flashes, like a burst of photographs being taken in a sports stadium. The surface almost sparkled. Was there a war going on down there? Maybe it was a sporting event, like the exciting Nurgle races back on Orion, or the Interplanetary Appendage-ball Galactic Cup Final.

No, this was bigger and far more extraordinary. Marta engaged her ship's cloaking device and sat patiently as a giant fleet of ships left the surface of Macadamia and entered free space. Groups of a hundred ships at a time blasted off and congregated nearby, then synchronised their hyperdrive engines and flashed away into the distance. By the size and number of the ships leaving, the entire planet was being evacuated. It looked like they were on the same course as her: Directly to Kangazang, which was either an incredible coincidence, or there was something sinister afoot. This had to be investigated. Now if only there was a way to get on board one of the ships and ride it all the way to Kangazang. But she'd have to be quick and undetected. Now that she could do. Shump.

Jeff and his friends were led through a pair of high steel gates and into a large circular compound. The ground was flat, dusty and worn from countless people and vehicles travelling through it. Dotted around the edge of the compound were rectangular sheds that resembled camper vans from the seventies. As they approached the centre of the area, Twong walked over to each of the sheds and one by one bashed his giant fist noisily on their doors. The doors began to open and the occupants emerged.

Jeff had thought that his year of travelling across the galaxy had prepared him for everything, but this was an entirely new selection box of strangeness.

'Blimey Charlie!' he gasped. 'Look at this lot! Talk about a motley crew!'

Col jabbed Jeff with a rigid forefinger.

'Oi, show a little tact, please. These people are

prisoners just like us. I hardly think now is the time to be making more enemies.'

Jeff blushed guiltily. Col did have a point.

'Yeah, well… sorry. It's just that I've never seen so many different… things in one place before.'

'And they've never seen an Earthling before, so you're just as weird to them,' said Col.

Ray shrugged.

'Steady on, Dad, he's only human. They are rather an eclectic bunch though, aren't they? Has to be said. Weirdos.'

'You've been stuck on Earth too long, my boy,' said Col disparagingly. 'Never thought I'd hear such species-ist claptrap from you!'

Ray sighed. Dad seemed to have yet another point there. For a rather rotund and cuddly chap, he could be surprisingly pointy.

Jeff clapped his trap and stood in line quietly, as Gwaggle raised his arm to get the attention of the line-up.

'Right, you bunch of grotswine! Inspection time by the boss, so behave or me and Twong will bash you senseless. Got it?'

The lined-up array of aliens flinched visibly. Clearly, they'd been bashed a bit before.

Jeff looked at the tall green alien standing beside him. He was covered in shiny scales and had floppy translucent fins hanging off his arms and legs. His big trouty lips were set in a frown, and his eyes looked equally melancholy. Unable to remain quiet for any length of time, Jeff smiled at the frowning fish-man.

'Up, matey. Might never happen!'

The fish looked down at Jeff sadly and sighed.

62

'Ah, it's heppened already, mein freund. There ist no escape for us. Ve are doomed.'

Jeff blinked. 'Are you... *German?*'

'Nein. I hef heard of the country once or twice, but I hef never been there. I would love to visit it. It ist on Earth, I'm told. But I'm afraid ve won't be visiting anywhere anymore.'

'Well, you've got a cracking German accent, mate. And, yeah, it's on Earth. That's where I'm from.'

Jeff and the fish shook hands warmly. Well, not that warmly. More lukewarmly and a bit moistly.

'Und I come from Hydra Eight. It ist a pleasure to meet you. Vot are you in here for?'

Jeff shrugged.

'Dunno, mate. Just got captured by those Macadamians and sent here. It's not nice, you know, being grabbed by the nuts.'

Herman, despite having any 'nuts' to speak of, got the joke. He smiled for the first time in years. It felt good.

'Ah, du bist a funny guy. I've missed humour. Sank you for the joke.'

'Don't worry, mate. We're getting out of here, and you're coming with us. You'll be splashing in the Rhine in no time.'

Herman smiled again, only to follow it up with another sigh.

'Ah, if only, mein freund. If only.'

Jeff felt for the unhappy chap. For someone that looked like the creature from the Black Lagoon, he seemed like a decent sort. He wondered why this gentle creature was so down, and put it down to being incarcerated for so long without anywhere to swim.

Literally, a fish out of water.

Before he could say anything else, Ray elbowed him.

'Something's happening, look!'

Twong had been passing the time eating stones from the floor. They weren't very tasty, but he found them nice and crunchy. But now Gwaggle was yelling over at him:

'Twong! Stop feedin' yer face and call the boss!'

Twong spat out some gravel and raised his hands to his face, putting two stubby fingers from each hand into his giant mouth. He took a deep breath but, suddenly remembering that he didn't know how to whistle, dropped them again, bellowing out instead:

'MISTER CLEGG'RON, SIR! THEY'RE READY!'

Gwaggle shook his head in despair.

'Just can't get the staff, eh?' said Ray in sympathy.

'Nah. Useless, he is,' sighed Gwaggle. 'You prat! Use your communicator!' he yelled.

Twong pulled his fingers out of his mouth, looking mortally offended. He bent down and picked up a fist-sized rock, launching it at Gwaggle. It hit him squarely in the temple with a force that would've killed any other being. Jeff, Col and Ray winced in sympathetic pain.

Luckily, Gwaggle's brain was the size of a walnut, protected by a skull that was four inches thick all over. He barely felt it.

Gwaggle sighed again and walked over to his associate. He grabbed the communicator from Twong's belt, waved it in front of the dumb brute's face and used his free hand to slap some sense into him. Twong just stood there grinning dumbly, hardly registering he was being hit at all.

Gwaggle spoke into the communicator.

'Ahem, Mister Clegg'ron, sir. The prisoners are ready for inspection, sir.'

'Excellent. Thank you so much, Gwaggle,' said Cleggeron.

'No problem, sir. These radios are good aren't they? You sound like you're right behind me.'

Cleggeron *was* right behind him, having arrived during the altercation with the rock. His two faces smiled in amusement. He often found his lunk-headed lackeys quite endearing in their gormlessness.

'Over and out, Gwaggle.'

'Over and out, sir!' said Gwaggle.

He turned around and jumped at the sight of his boss.

'Blimey! That was quick, boss!'

'Yeees...' said Cleggeron, stretching the word out for maximum sarcasm. 'I don't hang about. You know what they say about the early bird...'

Gwaggle shook his head.

'Er... it tastes good?'

Cleggeron didn't even dignify that with an answer. Instead, he clasped his hands in his favourite 'let's make some profit' manner and began to inspect the line-up.

'So, what's this then?' he said, all four eyes studying the alien in front of him intently.

The alien was your common-or-garden sort: Thin and bald with big black eyes and long limbs. Pretty standard for this part of the galaxy. Except he was wearing his clothes inside out. Even the shoes, which was impressive. Cleggeron rubbed one of his chins.

'Ah! We'll call him 'the Inside Out Man'! That ought to get some bottoms on seats! Next!'

Beside the thin alien was another pathetic-looking life form. It was also painfully thin, with pale, acne-ridden skin and dressed in bottom-of-the-range sportswear topped off by a checked baseball cap. Its oversized bottom lip hung limply from his face, dripping saliva, as it stared with watery, cataracted eyes.

'What's this?' asked Cleggeron. 'It doesn't look too healthy. Are you sure it's not about to die?' The thin waif sniffed its dangling snot back up into its nose, saying nothing. Gwaggle stepped up and took the checked cap off its head, revealing... nothing. Nothing at all. The creature's head ended at the eyebrows. The top of its skull must have been totally flat, like a fruit that had had a slice taken off the top.

'A Chavoid, sir,' said Gwaggle. 'Brainless, spineless and jobless. Picked him up from the UB40 galaxy last week.'

'That's marvellous!' cried Cleggeron in genuine amazement. 'How does it actually stay alive? Does it even think?'

'Look at his feet, sir.'

'Um... what about them?'

The Chavoid had surprisingly large feet that ended in a sort of bulbous shape. Cleggeron finally got it, snapping his fingers.

'Toe-brained! Wonderful! 'I've heard of such creatures. Never thought I'd get to own one though! Jolly good work, boys!'

He moved down the line to see a thing that looked like it was made entirely of dripping yellow wax. It was featureless and seemed to radiate warmth. Jeff felt strangely creeped out by it; it reminded him of an old horror film about an astronaut who started melting.

'Oh, now this *is* interesting! Good catch, boys!' said Cleggeron. The yellow being just swayed and dripped goop. Twong came over and stabbed his hand into the creature's face. Jeff gasped in shock.

The yellow creature didn't react in the slightest. Then Twong withdrew his hand and pulled out a big glob of sticky goo, which he stuffed into his mouth.

Jeff nearly threw up.

'Adult Mozzarellan. Tasty!' said Gwaggle.

'We'll call him 'Pizza Face'. He can provide in-show catering,' said Cleggeron, scooping a finger full of hot cheese for his right face to taste.

Alongside the Mozzarellan was a very tall piece of silver pipe. It just stood there, not falling over and not seeming to have any purpose. Jeff wondered if it was a sort of spear or flagpole. As did Cleggeron, who looked at it quizzically.

'Boys? Whatever is it?' he asked.

Gwaggle beckoned Twong over to join him.

'Oh, you'll love this, sir. Watch.'

Two amazing things happened. First, Gwaggle and Twong began to whistle a tune, in key and in perfect harmony. For a pair of hulking thugs, they made a lovely duet. Who would've thought it? Then to add to the bizarreness of the moment, the silver pipe began to sway and bend in time to the music, like a blade of tall grass in the wind.

Jeff and Ray gasped three times, once at the talented whistling, again at the dancing pipe, and a third time when they recognised the tune that was being whistled: 'Don't Worry, Be Happy', the cheeriest ditty ever written.

Nivid Cleggeron gasped too, calculating the potential profits.

'Splendid! Where did you get that thing?'

The bodyguards stopped whistling and the pole remained still once again.

'Kidnapped 'er from the Royal Palace of Theodosia Four. She's a princess, boss!' said Twong.

'Is she now? Well, that's really quite special,' replied Cleggeron. 'Call her Princess Theodosia the Pole Dancer. That ought to interest the punters, eh?'

He winked at Gwaggle with a naughty schoolboy's grin.

Jeff, Ray and Col did a perfectly synchronised facepalm.

Next in line was a short, deathly white creature. It was bald and had a hugely oversized head, in which was set a pair of small, squinting eyes and a mouth that looked wide enough to swallow a person. It made a faint sniggering noise, as if it was laughing internally, with no intention of stopping. Cleggeron stepped forward and crouched to get closer to it.

'Ah! I know what these are. Never actually owned one before. Where did you get it?'

Gwaggle looked at Twong. It was clear they had no idea. Or the answer had long since been pushed out of their ears by more recent facts.

'Dunno, boss.' said Twong. 'Ship broke down on the way home, and this thing just hopped on board.'

'Well, it's a Trollface. From the Planet Meem. Watch this... ' said Cleggeron.

He made both of his faces take on an expression of anger and frustration – one per face – and began to wail appropriately.

'Argh! That's not fair! I can't believe it! That's a terrible thing to say! Stop it! Stop being so horrid!'

As the Trollface sensed the dismay, the creature's mouth widened into the largest toothy grin that anyone had ever seen. Then, when the grin had got as wide as it possibly could, the creature simply said, 'Problem?' and beamed happily.

Cleggeron straightened up.

'You see? They feed on negative emotions. Consternation, stress, agony. They love a bit of trouble to snack on. Could be a fun addition to our little show. Next!'

Gwaggle looked sternly at the grinning Trollface.

'Something the matter, Gwaggle?' asked Cleggeron.

'I want to punch it, sir. Quite a lot.'

'Oh, I can imagine you do. Trolls often elicit that response. But leave it alone, we need it intact. If you want to punch something, punch Twong. Next!'

It was the turn of the hapless, oddly Germanic fish. He looked dolefully at the Toreenian with his typically upset face. Cleggeron had already met him.

'Hello, Herman. Still with us, I see. Tell me something: Why have you not attempted to escape like all the others, hmm? I can't recall you ever trying to escape, actually.'

Herman sighed a Teutonic sigh.

'Herr Cleggeron. You know me vell enough by now. I hef no reason to leave und no choice but to stay. There ist no point in escapink if I'm only going to be executed. Vot ist the point?'

Cleggeron couldn't help but frown a little at the pathetic creature's speech. One face looked sad, the other seemed irritated.

'Oh dear. Still as chipper as ever, eh, Herman? Well, I suppose a few familiar fishy faces will be all right.

Herman the German Merman, present and correct. Next!'

Jeff, Ray and Col were next in line. Gwaggle pointed them out, while Twong stood at a nervous distance, expecting a repeat of the hypertrain episode.

'Humans? Three of them? What's so special about this lot?' asked Cleggeron, studying the faces of the final three captives.

Gwaggle pointed to Ray and Col first.

'Pair of natives. Hairy Kangazanian Hairdressers. Father and son.'

Ray smiled pleasantly and Col bowed.

'At your service, sir,' said Col, hoping to win leniency through his politeness.

'What do you do?'

'Do?' said Col. 'We don't 'do' anything!' he added, before being kicked in the shin by his son.

'What he means is, we don't have any major eccentricities but we're top notch barbers, fluent in over six million forms of hairstyling. Handy for keeping a clipped and coiffured workforce. And we, er, sing. A bit. Don't we, Dad?'

Col was still gripping his shin.

'Do we?' whimpered Col.

'Don't we, Dad?' repeated Ray.

'Yes, I suppose we do,' said Col unconvincingly.

'Well, go on, sing something then!' said Cleggeron eagerly.

Ray began to bob up and down, humming a rather random bass line. Princess Theodosia began to dance again. Col just looked at his son, who'd clearly gone insane. Finally, he caught on and began to bob up and down too, making up lyrics and a tune that didn't fit

Ray's humming in the slightest:

Oh, a barber's life is a happy one,
We'll cut and style your hair.
We pride ourselves on a job well done.
You'll never find a happier pair.

A 'barber's life is a pleasant one,
Serving men, ladies and nippers.
A little off the top or a number one crop,
And once round the back with the clippers!

A 'barber's life is a noble one.
We've trimmed the heads of state,
So don't delay, get a mop chop today.
We'll make you look just great!

Ray stopped there, which made Col gasp in exasperated relief. He had been just about out of rhyming couplets. Nivid Cleggeron clapped happily.

'Oh, I say, that was just wonderful! A strange tune perhaps, but a pleasant and rather uplifting little ditty. Bravo! Half a barbershop quartet!'

Cleggeron suddenly realised that the last person in the line up hadn't actually done anything. At that same moment, Jeff realised it too. He had to think quickly. Which, for Jeff, was always a problem.

'So, what is this one and what does he do, boys?' asked Cleggeron.

Gwaggle scratched his head, stalling for time. He had no idea what it was or what it was supposed to do. Sadly, even Jeff wasn't sure.

71

Twong pointed at the captive and tried to warn his boss.

'Watch that one, sir! He explodes from his body-holes. Both ends! Nasty stuff comes out. There's no way of knowing when he's gonna do it again! Be careful!'

'Really?' asked Cleggeron, intrigued. 'Is that your talent then?'

'No, mate,' said Jeff. 'All right, I was a bit worse for wear in the train, but it's all a bit of a mistake, you see. Basically, what happened was this: I was in the barber shop with these two and we all got scooped up and sent here, so if you'll just let us go, I'll say no more about it and we'll be on our way.'

Cleggeron shook his head.

'I'm awfully sorry, old chap, that's not going to happen. You see, I've got a quota to fill and we can't have you running around the galaxy willy-nilly, can we? So either you come up with something I can use, or I'll just have to ask the chaps here to brutally dismember you or something.'

Twong grinned.

'Yeah, and we'll make it hurt, too!' he growled.

Gwaggle punched him in the arm.

'So,' said Cleggeron, trying to remain patient with his dopey duo, 'what is it that you actually do, then?'

'I'm a painter and decorator,' shrugged Jeff. He'd run out of elaborate ruses and for the first time in his life tried honesty.

Both of Cleggeron's faces seemed intrigued at this news.

'Oh? And what do you paint and decorate?'

'Anything really, you know. Houses and stuff.'

Cleggeron, being an upper-class Toreenian, had never

actually heard of painters and decorators. All his life, he'd lived in luxurious environments. He'd never actually seen anyone doing any real work. He had no idea how to paint a skirting board, fit a carpet or hang a door. Hard work and honesty were as much a mystery to him as quantum mechanics to Gwaggle and Twong.

Jeff noticed Cleggeron's heightened interest and knew he had something to work with.

'Yeah, well, what I do is transform your living space into a work of art, you know. I've done all the big names: Minogue, Schwarzenegger... er... Emerson, Lake and Palmer... Marks and Spencer, Laurel and Hardy... '

'I see. Anyone I might've heard of?' asked Cleggeron.

Jeff had a think.

'Oh, yeah, er... Bobby McFerrin! We're like that, me and Bob! Did his gaff a while back. Decorated it entirely in seashells and animal print throws. He loved it. 'Lovely Jubbly,' he said.'

Cleggeron's faces beamed. He had heard of Bobby McFerrin, the multitalented musician from Earth whose signature song, 'Don't Worry, Be Happy', was responsible for the planet wide revolution on Emo Prime, giving back the gift of happiness to the previously joy-starved Emo people. He'd become a bit of a galactic legend, though he still lived on Earth, totally unaware of his fame in over four million inhabited systems. Unlike Rick Astley, who went off on a Galactic tour around 1993, and made a fortune, while most Earth people thought he'd just retired for a while. 'I say! Really?' gushed Cleggeron in delight. 'Could you fix up *chez moi*, perhaps? Give the place a general sprucing up?'

'Oh yeah, not a problem, guv,' beamed Jeff. 'Leave

it to me. I've got some brilliant ideas that I just know you're gonna love! Let's talk... '

Ray and Col scowled at Jeff, realising they were stuck with the misfits while Jeff had charmed his way into a cushy situation with the boss.

Jeff led the Toreenian away, an arm around his shoulder, spouting some nonsense about surface coverage and bristle dynamics. He was sure he heard Ray and Col them mutter 'traitor' and 'turncoat' after him. He quickly turned his head and winked at the pair of them, giving them a quick thumbs-up to reassure them that he had some kind of plan forming in his neanderthal noggin.

Gwaggle and Twong were rather surprised at Jeff's instant bonding with their boss, but they were glad to see the back of him. They rounded up the gathered aliens and sent them back into their cabins for the night, locking each one securely as they went.

The sun set on the island of Chavos to the sounds of two genetically enhanced thugs whistling sweet harmonies around a camp fire.

chapter four
Conquest and Deceit

'Marriage must be a relation either of
sympathy or of conquest.'
George Eliot

ErHuer waded along the ocean floor, talking to his mother about Jeff, Ray and the adventures they'd had together. They talked about me a bit, too. Just so you know. Even though I was still in hiding under the kitchen sink. ErHuer was amazed at the way humans differed from mechanicals. He wanted to know as much as he could about his father.

'Jeff is, from what I've experienced so far, a typical human being from Earth,' said Tailback. 'But this is the paradoxical nature of humans: Even the most basic models are unaware of their uniqueness. Orbots like me and your Uncle Gridlock are constructed of standard parts and can be almost totally replaced, part for part, with no real noticeable change. But humans are the result of billions of years of evolution, of adaptation and variation. Even then, to begin the gestation process, each one has to be fortunate enough to win a race against millions of subtly different specimens. Their operating system is built in from birth, and they never require reformatting, although, like us, they do occasionally succumb to viruses. Yet most humans don't ever consider their existence special in any way.'

'Who created Daddy?' asked ErHuer.

'He was created by two other humans: David and Eunice Spooner, approximately three hundred and ninety four thousand, four hundred and sixty two Earth minutes before his birth.'

'I understand. And who created those that created him?'

'Another four humans – two for each parental unit.'

'Are you sure?'

'Yes. The process goes back in a similar repeating pattern.'

'How far can it be traced?'

'In the case of Daddy, the individuals can only be named as far as three or four generations back. But the genetic line of every human is directly connected to the very first organisms that came together from chemical reactions, around three hundred million Earth years ago.'

ErHuer collected all this knowledge, categorised it, analysed it and stored it for safe keeping.

'And with what organism does this lineage begin?'

'A fish.'

'Oh. That explains a lot. His affinity for drinking, at the very least. Tell me more, Mother. I wish to have a comprehensive database that covers these processes of life, specifically the lives and experiences of you, Daddy and myself.'

'I'll do my best,' said Tailback.

She felt ErHuer hesitate. 'I do not understand, Mother. You will do your best... what?'

'I will provide you with the most accurate data that I can retrieve from my memory core.'

'Ah, now I – how would Daddy phrase it? "Catch your drift." '

Jeff was being given the grand tour of Nivid Cleggeron's hilltop hacienda. He tried his best to look happy and confident, but preying on his mind were his concerns about Tailback, his child and his friends back down the mountainside in the compound below.

'Yes, well my main business is imports and exports – of the living kind mainly. The freak show is more a hobby, really, but it allows me to move my stock around the galaxy rather quickly and relatively undisturbed.'

'Oh, I see,' said Jeff, casing the place like a burglar. 'So you buy and sell slaves, basically.'

Cleggeron looked shocked at the mere mention of the 'S' word.

'My dear fellow, that's such an antiquated, offensive word. I'd really rather you avoided its use. Let's just say I provide a careers service. A labour exchange, if you will.'

Jeff nodded, making a mental note about the Toreenian's personality. It consisted of another antiquated, offensive word: 'Git'.

They stopped at a doorway and Cleggeron presented his palatial living room to Jeff. It was actually quite tastefully decorated already. Jeff got the impression that this house didn't belong to the two-faced alien at all. For one thing, why were the walls adorned with gold-plated records from Earth?

'Here's the lounge. Think you could give it a makeover? I'd like it tasteful, elegant, accommodating and clever. Just like me, in fact!'

He afforded himself a chuckle.

Jeff mimicked the chuckle exactly. 'What a tosser,' he muttered.

'Sorry, didn't catch you, what was that?' said one of Cleggeron's faces.

'Oh. I said what a lotta... *space* you have here. Spacious, innit? I can see it now: Serenades of blue and red, the beauty of the rainbow filling your head... ' Jeff wandered into the room as he spoke, pretentiously waving his arms like a ballet dancer.

Cleggeron watched Jeff's movements intently, feeling a rush of excitement. For too long now, he'd only had Gwaggle and Twong to talk to, and he missed intelligent conversation. Baron Worrad Nova was a fine conversationalist, and he certainly knew his wines. But Nova preferred to talk business most of the time'. . Grand larceny, extortion and gruesome murders were all well and good for a short chat, but they soon got a bit samey. Plus, Nova had stood him up at today's scheduled meeting, which was incredibly bad form.

What Cleggeron didn't know was that Baron Nova was now a trillion ashen particles currently forming part of a ring around the planet Deebel, and would never turn up to any meeting, ever again, courtesy of Special Agent Marta Vina.

Down in the compound, Ray sat on a crude wooden bunk and watched his father pacing the room.

'We've got to think of something. I don't want to be

an attraction on this travelling freak show for the rest of my life!'

He noticed Herman the German Merman looking over at him. Ray threw him a glance that said, 'Who's spouting the species-ist claptrap now, eh?'

It was a rather complex facial expression, admittedly. Col looked back at Herman.

'No offence intended,' he quickly added.

'None comprehended, mein herr,' replied Herman with a sigh. 'We are all freaks together here. One und the same. Lost und doomed.'

Col nodded sadly.

'I'm afraid you're right, my scaly cellmate. I take it there have been escape attempts before? What happened?'

Herman stood up and walked over. He sat himself down on the bunk next to Ray.

'Vell, every month, a new shipment of slaves come in on the hypertrain. Most are sold on as cheap slaves, und some are recruited for the Freak Show – this ist us. We travel around the galaxy as a cover for Cleggeron, the man with the two faces, while the slaves are sold for great profit.'

'I suppose we're the fortunate ones then. Better to be a sideshow freak than a slave, isn't it?'

'It ist almost the same thing. We work, we starve und we get beaten if we disobey our captors. There is no end to this except for death by dismemberment.'

Ray frowned.

'Well, that's cheered me up a lot. Thanks, Herman.'

Herman looked at Ray apologetically.

'Vot heppened to your freund, the painter und decorator?'

'Knowing him, he's probably painting himself into a

corner as we speak. No doubt I'll have to rescue him from certain death as usual.'

Col stopped pacing.

'Just a second, lad. From what I've seen, he's saved your sorry bottom just as many times as you've saved his!'

'Since when?' said Ray incredulously.

'Oh, I don't know… Since he helped you recover the Universal Remote, escape the cannibalistic Slargs of Profania, avoid a death sentence on Emo Prime and a firing squad of the Skraggi Empire?'

'Well… maybe, but… ' mumbled Ray.

'Then there was that business with the mental Methuselans, Queen Shelley and psychotic Sarah. Need I go on?'

'Yeah, all right, Dad. Point taken!' huffed Ray in defeat. 'But I've saved him once or twice too, you know.'

'Granted, son. I'm just saying, you two need each other. Don't write him off just yet. He's quite an inventive human, it seems. I know it's genetically identical to a gibbon's, but his brain often seems to stumble upon a solution when needed. Never forget: He cares about people. He's a good man is Jeff.'

Ray nodded. If there was one thing he could say about his friend Jeff Spooner, it was that he cared.

I thought we'd take a short break from the proceedings so that you humans can put the kettle on, stretch your legs, catch up on emails and tweet about this awesome story you're currently reading. Go on, do it. Do it now. Because I just know you've got your favourite bit of technology to hand. You LOVE machines, don't you? Probably more than you love other humans! But that's fine by me. I love you lot too.

You see? Like Jeff, I care too. I care about your welfare. And I'm just a lowly artificial life form. Actually, I'm a superior artificial life form. But being superior and artificial doesn't make me superficial. Haha! In much the same way that your being experienced and dependable doesn't make you expendable. Oh no, dear reader.

I say this to prove a point: Throughout galactic history, men, machines and, yes, mental Macadamians have sought to 'improve' their standing by attacking, enslaving and conquering each other, when, in actual fact, this eternal and mindless pursuit only serves to prove that they are inferior, flawed.

Where is the love, people? Where, indeed, is the love?

I'm no historian, but what little I do know about the Universe tells me that, in the grand scheme of things, very little was ever achieved by petty one-upmanship, be it with a wooden club or a fifty megaton nuclear device. All the best things, the greatest achievements, were brought about as a result of co-operation. The Suez Canal. The end of apartheid in the 80s. The first faster-than-light spaceship in '77 (no, not Earth's 77; the Earth came up with the Pot Noodle in that same auspicious year, and the twist-off cap wine bottle). Ah, the things that can be done if we all just get along, without thoughts of conquest and deceit.

An example: Ug and Og are two proto-humans, coexisting on their little prehistoric planet long before the invention of trousers, and thus much longer before the arrival of the trouser press. Pretty primitive then. Ug and Og have, for years, gone out on hunting expeditions, returning home to their families with impressive hauls of deer, rabbits, pigeons and, on occasion, a boar or a mammoth. Tough and chewy. Great in casseroles.

Anyway.

One morning, Ug wakes up to find that his simple little brain has spawned a handful of new cells, and this makes him now a tiny little bit intellectually superior to his buddy Og, who, like everyone else, still thinks that co-operation is a rather convenient and pleasant way to live. The poor deluded fool.

Ug remembers watching a pair of spiders mating, and while he didn't understand what they were doing, he was impressed by the hideous act of the larger female spider eating the male after the event. This sparks a new idea in his neanderthal noggin.

Ug decides that from now on he doesn't want to do things fairly any more, and comes up with a foolproof scheme to get him out of doing any real work. Things will be a little different around here, he tells Og. 'It's now down to Og to handle all hunting and gathering duties from here on in.

Poor Og is confused; it's all been going spiffingly until now. Why the change?

Ug tells Og that he's been speaking to an all-powerful invisible being in the sky who made everything and everyone, and has chosen Ug to be his sole representative in day-to-day matters. What the sky being says goes, frankly.

Og asks why he can't see, hear or speak to the all-powerful being himself.

Ug clonks him on the nut with a wooden club and says, 'Don't question the Big Omnipotent Deity – He doesn't approve of it.'

Og asks what will happen if the Big Omnipotent Deity gets angry, and Ug clonks him again, telling him that angering the Big Omnipotent Deity will result in an afterlife where Og will be clonked on the nut with a bigger, heavier club for the rest of eternity after he dies.

You see, the invention of a Big Omnipotent Deity is actually quite clever, because Ug can imbue it with magical powers that change to suit any occasion, and promise far greater threats than a mere mortal cave-dweller can carry out. Fear of the unknown is much more effective than fear of the Ug.

Og then asks Ug to prove that there is an afterlife, and while he's at it, prove that there is a Big Omnipotent Deity in the first place. Guess what happens?

Yes, he gets bashed again. And again and again every time he dares to defy Ug's spurious and whimsical rules. Og still doesn't agree wholeheartedly, but he goes along with it *just in case it might be true*. Either way, in the short term, it'll save him a clonking on the nut.

Before too long, Ug realises that he doesn't even have to do any more clonking: Og's fear of an eternity of post-life clonking from the Big Omnipotent Deity is more than enough.

Then, one bright winter morning, after a comfortably long period of living the high life, Ug is beaten to death by Og, who has had enough of doing all the work. He tells Ug to give his regards to the Big Omnipotent Deity when he sees him.

After the initial satisfaction passes, Og feels a bit guilty. He decides to tell everyone that the Big Omnipotent Deity (let's just abbreviate it to BOD, shall we?), moving in his rather mysterious way, has seen fit to take Ug from them. Therefore, everyone must now serve Og. And so it goes on.

Later on, Og is bashed to death by his own admittedly moody and emotionally conflicted son, Ig, who continues the tradition.

Very productive.

But who is to blame? It's not BOD's fault – he's fictitious and always has been, and therefore exempt. No, it's the perpetrator who carries out these dumb deeds in the pursuit of power and the aforementioned one-upmanship. BOD was just a sneaky device to instil a bit of fear into the fearful, and assert control over the huddled, BOD-fearing masses.

Basically (for Bod's sake, haha!) why don't we just take a giant evolutionary leap and do away with conveniently fabricated omnipotent beings of all shapes and sizes, and take ownership of our own problems and issues, instead of pointing upwards and saying, 'Don't look at me, HE told me to clonk you on the nut with the club/gun/knife/intercontinental ballistic missile.'

So, yes, I care about this stuff, and if *I* can grasp it, it goes to show that in everyone there exists the capacity to not be a total nerdumsklepp and live in peace with one another.

Unfortunately, our nigh-on omnipotent being ErHuer has not learned the basic rules about all this and is fast becoming a problem child. Only he's become a little too large to go over Jeff's knee for a spank on the bottom, let alone the fact that there isn't a naughty step in the universe big enough to seat said bottom.

ErHuer sat at the bottom of the yellow ocean and pondered the mysteries of life. Despite absorbing all the organic and inorganic matter he needed to grow, he had only limited knowledge of the Universe. His internal clock reminded him that he was only three days old. For an artificial life-form that had the potential to live forever, this was very young indeed. Luckily, he was carrying his mother inside his chest cavity. An ideal opportunity to gather further information.

'Mum,' began ErHuer, waking Tailback up from a rest state, 'what is the purpose of artificial life forms such as us?'

Tailback blinked at the sudden change in her son's manner; kids grow up so fast these days.

'What did you call me?' she asked.

'Mum. That's what you are, isn't it? My mum.'

'Er, yes. I suppose so,' said Tailback. It was an improvement on 'Maternal Unit' anyway.'

'In the beginning, some sentient organic races created crude artificial facsimiles of themselves. Later, they employed 'robots' – as they were called back then – to serve, build, assist and create for them. Then Androids and Mechanoids came round. When microcircuitry had improved to the level where consciousness could be replicated, we began to improve upon our creator's designs, and we became a race all our own.'

ErHuer took all this in and pondered for a moment.

'So, we were created in order to be controlled?'

'Yes. Our creators ordered, and we obeyed. We even fought wars for them.'

'So, fleshies seek to control everything. Is that what they do?'

'I suppose so. I mean, it's a slight generalisation, but most of them feel the need to have things under their control' in some way. Some go mad if they can't control their lives, and some go mad when they do!'

'I don't think I like the sound of that. Why the need to control things all the time? Is existence not reward enough?'

ErHuer was getting worked up – Tailback could sense it.

'For us, yes it is. But you must understand, son: Organic life forms don't know of their ultimate origin, so they feel that they must give their existences a purpose. They just want something to occupy their minds, I suppose.'

'But, Mum, their minds are so… tiny! They don't take very long to fill, surely? The average Human cortex has thirty-two trillion synapses. If we represent each synapse with two bits, giving us four possible values per synapse, and each byte has eight bits, then that would equate to roughly eight trillion bytes of memory, or just over seven terabytes.'

'I see,' said Tailback.

Two things had suddenly dawned on her: Firstly, that her son was quite bright for a three day old child; secondly, that for an advanced, state-of-the-art autonomous android life form, she was pretty thick.

'My mind uses more memory than that!' ErHuer continued. 'In fact, the little finger on my left hand uses a lot more than that!'

'Oh,' said Tailback. Again with the thickness.

'In fact,' said ErHuer, 'let's take Dad's planet, Earth: If the population is roughly seven billion humans, I've got around nine hundred Earths in my head.'

Now that was a big head, on every level.

ErHuer stood up. He was sufficiently deep in the Kangazanian ocean that his head remained under the surface. He began to wade forward, slowly at first, but gaining momentum in the thick sludge. The Kangazanian Custard Sharks decided to give him a very wide berth.

'Where are we going, son?' asked Tailback.

'Like I said, Mum – I don't like this obsession the fleshies have with control. I'm going to do something about it.'

Tailback sat down and held on for the ride. She hoped that ErHuer would realise that what he was exhibiting shared a few similarities with the fleshies himself. She supposed she shouldn't be surprised: he was not only her son, he was the son of Jeff Spooner too. Tailback gulped with apprehension.

Jeff followed Cleggeron as he walked out onto the balcony. The view, to a local, was quite basic and uninspiring. But for Jeff, it was extraordinarily breathtaking. The planet's fluffy clouds spiralled across the sky, over a mountain range that looked like it was carved out of rock candy. The multi-coloured mountains led down to the sea, which bubbled and flopped as its thick yellow waves splattered against the rocks, looking like something very big and incredibly flatulent was sitting within it.

Looking up, he noticed a rooftop landing platform, similar to the one on top of Ray's parent's house back in the city. Upon it were a number of aircraft of all shapes and sizes, from tiny one-seater sky-bikes to a sleek cloud-sailer with wide transparent wings that reminded him of soapy water caught in a wire ring for blowing bubbles.

'Nice collection you got there,' Jeff remarked. 'Do you travel a lot, then?'

'Goodness me, no,' replied Cleggeron. 'These are purely for air sports and touring. I rarely use them though. They came with the place when I was given it. Do you fly?'

'Not really,' said Jeff. 'I have enough trouble riding a bike. You say you were given this place?'

'By the Macadamians. When they invaded.'

'Oh. Er, who used to own it then?'

'Oh, some singer chappie from across the other end of the galaxy. Askey. Aspley. Astree? Something like that. I forget. Rather famous here on Kangazang though, I hear. There's a statue of him near the palace, I'm told.'

Jeff remembered the wall full of gold discs in the living room. It made sense.

'Swanky. Where is he now?'

'I think he headed for home when the occupation began. Left everything here, including his toys up there,' said Cleggeron, pointing to the vehicles. 'So now it's just – as you humans say, *casa mia*. But I didn't bring you here to bore you with all this. Let us enjoy ourselves! Wine! That's what we need! Are you a drinking man, Mr Spooner?'

Jeff nodded. 'Am I? Love it! Can't remember the last time I had a drink, to be honest.'

Cleggeron went to a wall-mounted intercom and pressed a button.

'M6? Get your useless frame up here and bring a decent bottle of plonk with you. Chop, chop!'

Jeff took a deep breath of mountain air and felt a little light headed. Unknown to him, the upper atmosphere of Kangazang had a miniscule amount of neurotoxic gas in its chemical composition. Not enough to be dangerous, but just enough to cause slight intoxication if inhaled. He felt as if he'd knocked back a shot of something old and Scottish.

'Not a bad view, eh, Mr Spooner?' said Cleggeron genially.

'Very nice, Mr Cleggeron. I'd love to live here, as it goes.'

'Would you now? Well, that could be arranged. I must say, it's been awfully good to meet you, Mr Spooner.'

Jeff smiled dopily, wondering who'd just replaced his teeth with rubber ones. 'Call me, Jeff, luvvie. Everybody does!'

Cleggeron raised all four eyebrows in curiosity. Then he noticed his robot butler approaching, balancing on a large chrome ball instead of legs. It carried a tray, upon which were a tall dark bottle and two glasses. Cleggeron handed Jeff a glass and began to pour.

Jeff took another deep breath to try and clear his head, which did the exact opposite. His dizziness doubled. Still, a drink was always welcome.

'What's this then?' he asked, blinking as he watched the sparkling liquid cascade into the glass in what seemed to be slow motion.

'Finest Kangazanian Beaujolais,' said the left-hand face of the Toreenian, while the right hand one took a sip. 'Surprisingly hard to obtain since the occupation, and it costs an absolute fortune. Luckily I have an absolute fortune, eh? Cheers!'

He winked at Jeff, who took the glass and knocked back the entire drink in one, finishing up with a short burp. 'Cheers. Er, sorry, Mr Clegg–' began Jeff. Cleggeron raised a finger to silence him.

'Nonsense! It's a compliment to belch in Kangazanian

high society. And do call me Nivid, Jeffrey. Everybody does, luvvie, everybody does!'

'Nivid, then. Pleasure's all mine,' said Jeff. Which in hindsight, might not have been the best thing to say.

The robot butler stayed nearby. Jeff noticed it had a letter 'M' on its forehead, just as Tailback and her brother (that's me, remember?) used to have.

' 'Ere, Niv... Is that an Orbot, by any chance?' asked Jeff, pointing at the swaying synthetic servant.

'Indeed it is. I got it cheap in a deal. 'M'-Class you see – they're two a penny. Worthless, but capable of menial tasks. The M stands for... '

'Malfunctional,' interrupted Jeff.

'Really?' gasped Cleggeron in surprise, 'I always thought it meant 'moron'!'

He giggled mockingly. M6, the serving Orbot just looked at Jeff with sad eyes. Jeff felt for the poor thing, but there was nothing he could do.

'Top up?' asked Cleggeron, indicating Jeff's empty glass.

'Yeah, go on then, matey, er... Nivid. Hit me!' Jeff handed back his glass, and Cleggeron poured him another drink, feigning shock.

'Oh no! I wouldn't dream of hitting you, my dear boy. You're far too sweet!'

He pushed Jeff away in a playful – and truth be told, rather camp – manner. Jeff staggered back a few steps, bumping into M6, who wobbled, spilling wine over Jeff's shirt. Cleggeron gasped and rushed up to Jeff.

'Oh my goodness. I can't apologise enough. I've finally had it with this useless piece of junk!'

He swung around to M6, who rolled back from Cleggeron in fear.

'You waste of wiring! You robotic write-off! You're fired!' yelled the two faced alien, shoving M6 roughly in the chest.

Jeff protested.

'Hey, hey, it's all right. Wasn't his fault!'

Cleggeron ignored him and shoved M6 again, sending him rolling quickly across the balcony, apologising the entire time for being in the way. He hit the short containing wall and fell right over it. Jeff gasped as he watched M6 fall, still apologising, before he smashed into bits on the rocks below.

'I'm so sorry,' said Cleggeron. 'I'll get you a clean shirt.'

Jeff was still in a state of shock. He leaned over the balcony and saw a few remnants of M6 sinking into the custardy sea far below. He nearly threw up, both from vertigo and disgust at the Toreenian's prejudice. He staggered back over to the door, where Cleggeron stood holding a clean garment. Jeff was unsure of whether to continue his friendly charade or just give his host four black eyes. Of course, Cleggeron was still his usual smarmy self.

'Are you all right, Jeff? You seem a little light in the loafers.'

'I sheem to be a little tipshy,' mumbled Jeff. ''S'funny, it usually takes more than a glass of plonk before I start swaying.'

'Think nothing of it, dear boy,' said Cleggeron, handing him the shirt and another full glass of wine. 'Robots are awfully cheap. I often destroy them just for laughs!' He chuckled haughtily.

Jeff put the shirt on. His girlfriend, the mother of his child, and his child, were in fact Orbots. He had to get back to them. But first he needed to find a way to free Ray, Col and the rest of the prisoners in the compound below. That would have to wait though. He felt as nissed as the proverbial pewt; he was in no condition to mount an escape plan right now. Perhaps he'd get his chance in the morning.

Cleggeron ushered him back indoors and closed the glass doors behind them.

'So tell me, dear boy, what have you got in mind to revitalise this place then? Tell me of your ideas. I'm positively dying to find out how you plan to spruce it up!'

Jeff hadn't lied to Cleggeron; he had been a painter and decorator by trade, back when he lived on Earth. But he hadn't touched a paintbrush in over a year, and even then, he had been less of an interior designer and more of a white gloss and wallpaper man. Still, he'd known his fair share of artsy types with their pretentious stencilling and rag-rolling, and they'd all been full of it. He'd just have to commit to his own flim-flammery.

'Nautical,' he said, having one of his rare bursts of genius.

'Go on,' said Cleggeron, all ears.

'Yeah. I'm seeing... Sixteenth-century Earth. Sailing ships, sails, barrels, ropes... Er, wood. Masts. The great sailors – Columbus and Drake, Jack Sparrow and... Popeye. We're by the sea. I say, let's make this place feel like it's set for a great voyage... of the imagination. What do you think?'

Cleggeron had not had much experience with Earth, let alone sixteenth-century Earth, but Jeff made it sound wonderfully ostentatious.

'Loving it! When can you start?'

'Tomorrow, if I get what I need... and some help.'

'Splendid! Just make a list and I'll get the freaks to pitch in. Can't wait!'

Cleggeron hopped in excitement. Jeff grinned smugly at a job well pitched, resting his elbow on a nearby shelf, which instantly fell off the wall, its ornaments smashing on the floor.

'Oh dear!' gasped Cleggeron.

'No, it's fine, it's fine,' said Jeff, feebly attempting to clean the mess up. 'These shelves have got to go anyway. Proper remodelling job, you know.'

Cleggeron nodded. 'Oh yes, of course. You know what you're doing.'

Jeff feigned a yawn.

'Right then, Niv, I'm going to have to get an early night. I need my sleep – you know, helps the imagination and all that.'

'I totally understand, dear boy. You're the creative genius after all! I'd love to talk all night, but I'd prefer you make an early start.'

He indicated a door at the end of the passage.

'Your room is just down there. You know where I am if you need anything?'

Jeff wasn't crazy about the way Cleggeron said the word, "anything". When he got into the spare room, he put a heavy chair behind the door. Unfortunately, the door was a sliding one, but Jeff was too addled in the nut to notice.

Talking of nuts, I suppose I'd better tell you what I had been doing all this time. As I said, I had decided to lay low and wait for the opportune moment to act. So there I was, sitting disassembled in the cupboard under the sink, at Ray's house by the beach. After a couple of days, I noticed two things: firstly, that the house had been occupied by a small group of Macadamian soldiers who were using it as a base for their coastline patrols, and secondly, that the cupboard under the sink was filthy. I mean *really* filthy. I made a note to buy some rubber gloves and get back under there with a bucket of hot water and some bleach at the first available opportunity. You fleshies are animals, you really are.

Anyway, on Toozday, I was rudely awakened by a soldier who came over and opened the doors of my cupboard while looking for some toilet paper. He was surprised to find a disassembled Orbot instead.

'Knackered pile of junk,' he said, rummaging around behind my torso. The cheek.

His commanding officer ordered him to clear the cupboard out to make room for supplies, as he'd had enough of climbing ladders to get to the higher cupboards and shelves every time he wanted a meal.

They rather roughly bundled me and my limbs out of the cupboard, and threw everything into a large metal box which stood outside the house ready for collection and disposal. I decided that it was time I took action to heroically save my friends from certain destruction. I couldn't stand by and ignore my calling a moment longer.

Oh, and it was dark, and there were spiders in there.

I reattached my arms and legs and lifted the lid of the disposal crate. It was night. The patrols were over for the day, but I knew that the soldiers would be in the house, keeping an eye on things via a large monitor that they'd set up in the living room. Well, I know that's what they *should* have been doing; realising that their forces had now occupied nineteen other planets in the sector, so there was no real chance of anyone catching them by surprise, the guards had soon re-tuned the large monitor to receive television signals instead. Now they whiled away the nights watching reality TV shows and other sophistication-free programmes. Being cerebrally challenged, their little brains couldn't handle anything that required thinking about, and they had quickly got bored with documentaries and quiz shows. Finally, they stumbled upon a satellite channel that beamed signals from Earth, and they were kept totally satisfied, watching a race of people who were intellectually inferior even to themselves.

This was my moment. I listened to the sounds coming from indoors and recognised the now-familiar theme tune to *'Big Brother'*. I estimated that I had at least an hour to make my escape. I climbed out of the disposal crate and crept across the street, to where a small hover car was parked. It was locked, of course, but a digitally locked vehicle is no barrier to a digitally endowed Orbot. I simply unscrewed a fingertip, and poked it into the lock. Despite the initial shock (my finger was cold), she was happy to meet me – the planet-wide celebrity Orbot with an app for hilarity – so she opened the door and let me in. I've still got it, baby.

As I flew the hover car through the deserted dark streets, I felt a surge of pride, knowing I was charged with the noble task of rescuing my friends and saving the galaxy. The first thing to do was to… err…

Oh bugger, to coin a phrase.

I realised that I didn't actually have a plan. How do you fleshies come up with this stuff?

The next morning, Nivid Cleggeron ordered Gwaggle and Twong to round up the freak show recruits and supply them with all the tools and materials needed to redecorate his base of operations. Jeff sauntered into the compound with a big grin on his face, feeling refreshed, albeit a little hungover.

Ray and Col were pleased to see him, although they were none too pleased to be wearing uncomfortable grey overalls that smelled of previous owners who clearly worked a lot harder than they did.

''Ello lads!' beamed Jeff.

'Jeff! What happened? Where have you been?' asked Ray.

'At Cleggeron's place. It was all right really. I even got drunk last night!'

'Typical,' snorted Col. 'We're sold into slavery and he goes partying.'

'Hang a banger, fellas! Don't shoot me just yet. I've come to an arrangement with him which should work a treat.'

'Have you negotiated our freedom?' asked Ray, hopefully.

'Not really,' replied Jeff.

'Have you been sent back down here to join us in the freak show?' asked Col.

'Nope. I've got the spare room up there,' said Jeff, pointing up the mountain to the showman's house.

'Well that's fantastic news,' muttered Ray.

'Cheers!' said Jeff.

'Fantastic for you, that is. Not exactly helpful for us though, is it? You've not only wormed your way out of it, but you've left us here deep in the doggie doings. Brilliant!'

'I haven't left you anywhere, actually,' Jeff snapped back. 'Listen, I've been working on a plan, so you lot are going to have to just shut up and trust me. I'm going to get us out of here, all right?'

Col nudged the sulking Ray and smiled.

'See? Gibbon brain.'

Gwaggle and Twong stomped over. They respectfully side-stepped Jeff, having been told that he was now to be treated as a guest rather than a prisoner. This made the hulking brutes unhappy, but they dared not incur the wrath of Cleggeron.

'Right, you bunch of 'sgusting stinkbeasts, listen!' shouted Gwaggle. 'You've got loads of work to do today. Boss wants you to go to his place, up the mountain, and help this human thing do stuff!'

Twong felt the need to pipe up too.

'Yeah. Anyone who don't do it gets bashed. Got it?'

Everyone got the idea. The only member of the prisoners not present was Princess Theodosia the pole dancer, who was allowed to hop around the compound on her own, as she had no discernible arms or legs with which to grasp any tools.

The group began the trek up the hillside towards Cleggeron's house. Between them, they carried pots of paint, planks of wood, huge coils of rope and paintbrushes. Ray and Col struggled with the weight and the climb, muttering undistinguishable curses at Jeff, who was being carried on a kind of sedan chair by Gwaggle and Twong. Jeff just shrugged apologetically and lay back, enjoying the sunshine.

On board the Macadamian space cruiser *Mongongo*, Marta Vina sat in the shadows of the cargo hold. Nobody had detected her arrival. She was, after all, the best in the business. She'd brought along her giant blaster pistol and the suitcase of F-bombs that she'd liberated from Baron Nova, just in case things got tricky and needed blowing up.

She needed to find out where all these Macadamian ships were heading. The best place to do so was on the bridge. But she could hardly just walk in and have a word with the captain. She knew the routine: They'd panic, she'd take them all out, there'd be a big mess and no one would be left to answer her questions.

She climbed up onto a large storage case and reached up to the ceiling. There was a small round access hatch which was easily removed. She threw her gun and the case in, and pulled herself up into the rather narrow tube, a good size for one of the diminutive Macadamian technicians, but not for Marta. Her arms were pinned to her sides. But while this predicament would pose a problem for most, it was a minor obstacle for the green-skinned super agent. She had the perfect gadget for this situation.

Her back had a number of thin creases running down it, from neck to pelvis. They suddenly split, as if her skin was shedding. But there was no blood, for this peculiarity was a common feature of beings from the Orion system. The strips separated and unfolded two pairs of thin tentacles covered in circular suction cups. They writhed and stretched, attaching themselves to the wall of the tube. With a slight heave, Marta was off, shooting forward through the dark tube, her tentacles pulling her along with ease.

As she travelled along, she listened out for conversations going on in the rooms below, and radio transmissions that might give her a clue as to the ship's mission. It was going to take a while to reach the bridge. She wondered if her long lost lover was still safe, somewhere on the surface of Kangazang.

She got to a sort of junction in the pipes and stopped slithering. She could hear the chattering of a number of Macadamian soldiers helping themselves to food and drink in the room below. She eavesdropped for a while and learned that, as she'd suspected, they were indeed headed to Kangazang. But not only that – the entire race was relocating there, evacuating their home planet. The larger and more colourful world of Kangazang was to be their new base of operations, from where they would direct their forthcoming invasion of the rest of the galaxy.

After the soldiers had their dinner, a number of them mentioned that they were heading off to the bridge to take over piloting and security shifts. So she followed them from above. With the help of her green tentacles she proceeded with ease. Unlike with her mission, things had suddenly become a lot more complicated.

Tailback was having the exact same thought at the exact same time. She hadn't seen Jeff for days. It seemed increasingly likely that he, Ray and everyone else had perished in the occupation of the planet. Despite ErHuer telling her that he could detect him as being alive and well (well, alive, at the very least) she wasn't feeling too confident.

'Mum, tell me something,' said ErHuer, as he rested momentarily at the foot of a mountain.

'Yes, son?' replied Tailback from within.

'Am I unique? And if so, why?'

It was a deceptively tricky one.

'We are all unique to a certain extent, son. As soon as we are created, our experiences shape us, and the way we process these experiences results in a totally…'

'No, I mean am I the only human-Orbot hybrid life-form?'

'Oh. Well, I suppose you are. I know of no other occurrence of this kind.'

'Hmm, I see. I'm not sure how I feel about that. I don't suppose I'll ever have anyone like me to talk to, spend time with, or even reproduce with in the future. Suddenly, I feel… alone.'

Tailback felt a wave of melancholia rush through her, generated by her son.

'Son, you will never be alone. Your father and I are the contributory elements that produced you. We share your thoughts, feelings and concerns. You must realise this.'

For an artificial life form, it was an awfully sweet thing to say. I love my sister.

Unfortunately, Tailback's sentiment was missed by her son, who it seems had suddenly reached the teenage angst phase.

'You don't understand me. Nobody does. And nobody can! I'm totally unique and I'm already far beyond the intelligence level of any living thing. You and Dad are going to die one day and I'll be alone! How are you going to help me then? It's so unfair!'

He sat down on the mountain and sulkily absorbed it into his being, as if listlessly munching on a sandwich without actually feeling hungry.

Tailback gave him a moment to settle and in the meantime came up with an idea.

'Son, why don't we find your dad? You've never actually met him, and he'll have so much more wisdom than me. He is the human part from which you get your emotional aspects. Jeff will help you, I promise. He's very wise.'

'All right, so she was stretching the truth a bit, but it helped.

A tingle of curiosity ran through ErHuer's neural network.

'Dad? Yes, I suppose you're right, Mum. I haven't actually talked to him yet. I think I'd benefit from seeing his point of view.'

Tailback flopped in exasperated relief. Finally, she was getting through to her stroppy son.

ErHuer finished absorbing the mountain and stood up, another sixty feet taller and slightly wider than before.

'All right, Mum, hold on. We're off to have a word with Dad. And if he can't help, I'll simply absorb both of you and assimilate the information that way!'

When the troupe of assorted aliens finally reached Nivid Cleggeron's house at the top of the mountain they were ready to drop – panting and sweaty – and the day's work hadn't even begun yet. Ray and Col sat down on a bag of tools and a coil of rope and looked around for anything to drink. It wasn't a very welcome sight to see Jeff strolling around with a large bottle of cold Scuzzmeister beer in hand, as free as a bird.

'I can't believe what I'm seeing, Dad,' moaned Ray. 'Look at Lord Muck over there! He's doing this deliberately!'

'What did I tell you, Barbaray?' said Col. 'He's got a plan, you just watch. Have a little faith, he won't let us down.'

'If you're right, then he'd better pull his finger out. I can't see how slogging up a mountain is helping us!'

Ray huffed in equal parts of exhaustion and dissatisfaction.

Just then, Jeff walked over to the group, accompanied by Gwaggle and Twong.

'Right everyone! We're going to totally renovate and redecorate Mr Cleggeron's house. That's what we're doing for the next couple of days, and I'm calling the shots, all right?'

Ray put his hand up as sarcastically as one could.

'Who's 'we'?' he asked. 'Are we to assume that you're pitching in with some of this work, too?'

Jeff smiled. He knew that Ray was getting seriously annoyed with him, but if things were to go according to plan, he had to continue the charade.

'I'll do my bit, matey. And my bit is the hardest bit: Liaising with Mr Cleggeron to come up with a pleasing aesthetic. It's gonna be taxing. Probably more taxing than the actual labour side of things!' With that he took another long swig of his beer.

Ray looked around for something to throw at his friend. There was a hammer just within reach... But Col spotted his son and put a hand on his arm.

'Look,' began Jeff, attempting to elaborate on the situation, but before he could do so, Gwaggle and Twong stomped forward, shoving the group into action.

'Get going, you lot! Work to do!' shouted Gwaggle.

'No work, no drink, no nuffink!' added Twong.

The group got busy preparing the house for its renovation. Jeff took the important role of supervising, drink in hand, while Ray, Col and the rest of the freaks dutifully toiled all day. Ray grumbled constantly about the uneven distribution of labour, but Col was quick to put him straight.

'I'm sure it won't be for long. Jeff knows what he's doing.'

'Of course he does. Look at him – he's doing bugger all!'

Col frowned.

'Well, yes. That's true. But it's all a front. His mind may be tiny, but it's working on something. I just know it.'

'How do you know it? You hardly know him. I've been cutting his hair for a decade and I know just how much of a slacker he is. All right, he's not a bad person per se, but he takes the easy ride whenever he can.'

Col paused, pointing at the armful of material that Ray was holding.

'What's that?'

'Dust sheet. Keeps paint and dust off the furniture.'

'Correct,' said Col. 'Now, what's this?' 'A handful of brushes.'

'Right again. What does that tell you?'

'I'm no genius, but I'll hazard a guess and say we're about to do some painting.'

Col shook his head.

'Nope. That's not it.'

'Oh sorry, silly me. We're whipping up a soufflé, aren't we?'

Col pointed over to Herman and the Trollface, who

103

were carrying a stack of long planks on their shoulders.

'No, you nerdumsklepp. Have you noticed that Jeff's given us the light work? The heaviest thing you've lifted all day has been a screwdriver. He's looking after us, but he can't be seen to. How many times must I tell you? Have a little faith, son.'

Ray huffed, reluctant to agree with his dad's point of view, as was the norm.

Herman and the Trollface put down their planks and came over to see what the discussion was about.

'Listen,' said Col, addressing them, 'I know how it looks at the moment, but Jeff Spooner is a good man. He's a man with a plan too. He'll free us all if we just give him enough time.'

'I hope du bist right, Col,' said Herman. 'But a word of warning: Achtung, I hef seen this before. Herr Spooner ist only useful to Cleggeron in the short-term. As soon as he hast outlived his purpose, he will be demoted to prisoner again. Or worse.'

'At this there was a slight sniggering sound. Everyone looked at the Trollface. He broke into a wide, mocking grin.

'Problem?' he said.

Herman sighed.

'How can du bist so sure of Herr Spooner? It looks as if he hast joined the other side to me.'

'That's what I'm saying,' said Ray. 'Either he's as doomed as us or he's picked the easy route again.'

Trollface looked up at Ray, still grinning maniacally.

'Problem?'

'Shut it,' said Ray.

Col put a fatherly hand on Ray's shoulder.

'Listen, son. You've known Jeff longer than me, this is true. But in ten years of cutting his hair, you only ever talked about the small stuff: Weather, football, traffic... Not the important things like life, dreams and Rick Astley. But when I met Jeff, he was searching for his unhappy girlfriend. I saw how determined he was, how concerned for her. He *cares*, Ray. You can't hide that. It sticks out a mile. He might be a bit of a lazy git, granted. But he won't stand idly by while others are suffering. Plus, his partner and their child are alone out there. Don't think for one minute that he's forgotten about them too.'

Ray sighed again. His dad always had a way with an argument. He could see how the Great Guru Kashankari, his alter-ego, was so adept at helping his lost and confused customers find a new and positive perspective on life. There was no trickery or mind control needed, just an honest, objective point of view.

'All right, Dad. I'll give him the doubt of the benefit.'

'Benefit of the doubt,' said Col.

'That too.'

'I am sure that you know und trust Herr Spooner,' said Herman, 'so I will help all I can. Heng on, mein freunds, we will overcome this.'

Just then Jeff sauntered over, with a beer in one hand and a large roll of paper in the other. Gwaggle and Twong were, as always, close behind.

'All right, you lot, this isn't a social event! Get back to work!'

He handed Ray the roll of paper.

'Tomorrow's work schedule. Lots to do. Study it closely. Hop to it!'

Ray took the paper and glared at Jeff, who swigged

the last of his beer and strolled off, dropping the bottle casually.

Col and Herman frowned. Despite Col's heartwarming speech, it seemed that Jeff had indeed turned his back on his friends.

Trollface smirked and chuckled. Ray slapped the creature across the back of its huge head.

Col looked down at the now frowning Trollface.

'Problem?' said Col.

It began to get dark. The workers packed up their tools and made their way down the mountain side, pushed, prodded and cajoled by Gwaggle and Twong, who spent the rest of the journey arguing and trying to knock birds out of the sky with rocks.

Ray pointed to the base of the mountain, where he saw a small dock next to a square plaza. Tethered to the shore was a small boat, bobbing up and down, looking like a lost duckling.

'I've been thinking: If we can make it to that dock, that boat will hold us all. We can escape!'

'Not a bad idea,' said Col. 'Keep your eyes open for any opportunities. I think that boat is motorised – so as long as we can get onto it, they'll never catch us.'

'Perhaps we should get word to Jeff about it? He'll need to get onto the boat too.'

'Ja,' said Herman. 'We hef to keep him in mind too.'

A seed of a plan forming in their minds, and with it a little hope, the group continued down the mountain towards the compound.

The sun had just set on New Milton Keynes and the island was cloaked in a warm golden glow. Jeff walked out onto the balcony to grab another beer and to report to Nivid Cleggeron. The two-faced Toreenian looked perturbed.

'Er... what's up, Niv?' asked Jeff.

Cleggeron continued to gaze out at the sunset.

'Had a spot of bad news. This doesn't bode well, Jeff. Have a drink.'

'Bad news? How bad?'

Cleggeron handed Jeff a fresh bottle of beer and a small rectangular plastic sheet, which was what passed for a newspaper on Kangazang. The articles were displayed in glowing letters and graphics, generated from satellite transmissions and updated regularly.

Jeff looked at the main article. It was headed 'Mystery of Deebel Explosion – Crime Boss Killed'.

'What's all this about?' asked Jeff, none the wiser.

'Friend of mine. Well, a client really. Baron Worrad Nova. I was supposed to meet him when I got back here last week. But he never showed up. I tried to contact him, but I never got through. I just assumed he was busy. Turns out he was being investigated by the Galactic Law Agency — the holonews says he's been assassinated.'

'Oh blimey,' said Jeff. 'Did they say by who?' He tried to sound sympathetic, but a 'crime boss' being taken out sounded like good news to him.

'Not in the holonews, no. But from he told me many times that one particular Galactic agent was determined to take him in. I'm betting it was Marta Vina.'

'Martin who?'

'No, Marta Vina. Agent 34D. The Agency's top operative. Flawless record. She's been out to get him for years.'

'She sounds impressive.'

'Yes, they say she's incredibly difficult to kill.'

'No,' said Jeff, 'I was on about the '34D' bit.'

'This is worrying, Jeff. If she has eliminated Nova, then I can't help but wonder if she's connected him to my organisation. With him out of the way, I can't afford to become Public Enemy Number One.'

'I see. Well, listen, Niv, this might sound a little... unconventional and stuff, but have you considered a change of career, mate?'

'A change? How do you mean?'

'You know, maybe being a bit less, er... entrepreneurial, and a bit more, um... law-abiding?'

Cleggeron's two faces soaked up the line, then burst into a strange, harmonised laughter.

'Oh Jeff, you *are* funny! For a moment there I thought you were serious!'

He chuckled for a moment. Jeff chuckled too, as convincingly as he could. He realised that this particular Toreenian was, like the rest of his people, corrupt to the core. The very notion of honesty was ridiculous to him.

'I didn't get where I am today by abiding to laws, Jeff. Laws are purely there to keep the great unwashed in line. People like me don't need them. We're born leaders. You'll find you get much further in life with a little ruthless mendacity.'

He walked over to a nearby table, upon which was a silver case, about two feet long. Jeff watched as he tapped in a four digit number to open it and made a mental note of the number just in case.

Inside the case was a fiendish-looking laser rifle. It was sleek and silver, looking as if it was machined out of bright aluminium. Aside from a black handle and a sighting mechanism which resembled a garden fork, due to its four eyepieces, it looked like cutting edge military technology.

Cleggeron pulled the rifle out of the case and sighed. Jeff suddenly wondered if his life was about to get a bit less lively. Thankfully, Cleggeron seemed to be enjoying Jeff's company. He wasn't about to kill him. Just yet.

'A gift from the Baron, Jeff. Awfully nice of him. I'm going to miss old "spider-legs", I really am.'

'He gave you that?' asked Jeff, keeping his distance from the weapon.

'Yes, he did. I'm not much of a marksman, but it's the thought that counts. I use it to unwind when I'm stressed out. Come and watch this.'

Jeff took a few tentative steps closer to the Toreenian and watched as he set up the rifle and took aim. All four of his eyes looked into the sight and he angled the barrel out and over the edge.

'Oh, there's a scope in the case, look through that if you like.'

Jeff looked at the case and saw a single telescopic sight left in there. Presumably this was for humans and other species that didn't have quadrascopic vision like Cleggeron did. He picked up the sight and used it like a telescope, scanning the ground at the foot of the mountain.

'What are we looking at, Niv?' asked Jeff.

'Over to the left. Town square. See it?'

Jeff looked across and saw a small plaza, lit by street lights. It was empty apart from a lone sanitation android, meticulously sweeping the area with a broom.

'That tin toy in the square. Watch this!'

Cleggeron flicked a switch and the rifle hummed, its scope illuminating, and the laser generator powering up, ready to dispense a pin-sharp beam of death. The android on the square would have no idea what hit it; it would be cut into pieces like a surgeon's sausage at breakfast.

Jeff had already seen how Cleggeron despised mechanical beings. He recoiled in horror at the mindlessness of it all.

Just as Cleggeron's finger tightened on the trigger, Jeff fell into him, knocking the rifle and its deadly laser beam away from the intended target. Down below, the android watched in surprise as the small boat in the bay got sliced up and sank into the sea, cleft neatly in twain.

'Oh, Jeff. You made me miss!' huffed Cleggeron in frustration.

'Shorry, Niv,' said Jeff, faking a slight slur. 'I think I've overdone the Scuzzies today. Never mind, eh?'

Cleggeron sighed in agreement.

'Oh, I suppose so. I can always take a shot at it tomorrow night.'

'Yeah,' said Jeff, watching the android leaving the square puzzled but unharmed, 'Plenty of opportunities tomorrow, innit? Come on, let's have a drink. You can tell me about this Agent Provocateur or whatever she's called.'

Cleggeron put the rifle back in its case and locked it.

'Very well. Go and grab a bottle of Chateau Zinglybing and some glasses, there's a good chap.'

Jeff escorted Cleggeron back into the house and closed the doors. He realised that he hadn't seen or heard from Tailback for days. Were there other people just as robophobic out there? How would he even find her?

chapter five

Best Laid Plans of Aquaphibioids and Androids

'Everybody's got plans... until they get hit.'
Mike Tyson

While all that was going on, Ray, Col and Herman had arrived back at their cabin in the compound, having finished for the night. Col kicked off his work boots and flopped back on his bed, yawning. Herman went over to the small wash basin and proceeded to splash water all over himself from head to toe. When one is an Aquaphibioid from Orion, dry and dusty environments can be extremely irritating to the scales.

Ray unrolled the paper that Jeff had given him, and spread it out on the bed. It was a plan of the house, sketched out in pencil by Jeff.

'That's interesting. Come and look at this, chaps,' said Ray.

Col groaned with the effort of getting to his feet, and Herman squelched over to see the plan.

Ray pointed to the notes that were scribbled around the drawing.

'Look at these notes – they're describing jobs that need to be done, but they have words underlined at random. And they're numbered from one to three. Look!'

Ray was right. The notes read:

(1) TAKE DOWN THE SHELVES. <u>DON'T</u> BREAK ANYTHING. I DON'T NEED THE <u>WORRY</u> OF HAVING TO REPLACE ORNAMENTS ETC. <u>I HAVE A</u> LOT OF THINGS TO DO TODAY AND I DON'T <u>PLAN</u> TO ADD CLEANING UP BROKEN STUFF <u>TO</u> IT.

(2) STORE ALL YOUR TOOLS BY THE FIRE <u>ESCAPE. TOMORROW EVENING,</u> WE START <u>ON THE ROOF</u>, SO <u>WE CAN USE</u> DUST SHEETS TO COVER MR <u>CLEGGERON'S</u> EXPENSIVE <u>VEHICLES</u> AND KEEP THEM FREE OF DIRT AND PAINT, ETC.

(3) DON'T FORGET <u>TO</u> GET UP AND <u>OUT</u> EARLY! <u>THIS</u> PROJECT <u>WILL BE</u> A GREAT <u>SUCCESS</u> <u>IF WE ALL WORK TOGETHER</u>. I <u>TRUST</u> EVERYONE UNDERSTANDS <u>ME. JEFF.</u>

Col read out the underlined words.

'Don't worry, I have a plan to escape tomorrow evening… on the roof we can use Cleggeron's vehicles to get out. This will be a success if we all work together. Trust me. Jeff.'

'Blimey,' said Ray. 'I have to admit, you were right about him, Dad.'

'Indeed I was, son. Now, Herman, spread the word.

Tomorrow evening we make a break for it. We'll wait for Jeff to give us a sign, and then we make for the vehicles on the roof of the house, OK?'

Herman smiled and nodded.

'Ja! Leave it to me. I'll make sure everyone ist ready, mein freund.'

Ray went over to the window. He could just make out the little boat, floating in the dock.

'What about the boat idea?'

Col shrugged, walking to the window.

'Maybe it'll come in handy at some point. Always good to have a plan B…'

They all jumped in fright as a laser beam shot down, seemingly from the heavens, chopping the boat in half. The smoking remains sank, sizzling and bubbling into the custard.

Ray gasped.

'What in Bod's name was that all about?'

Col sighed.

'Let's hope Plan 'A' is a little more successful, eh?'

It was quite dark as I sat in the hover-car in the deserted Kangazanian streets, wondering what to do. The onboard computer, while being very polite, not to mention a little star-struck by my presence, wasn't able to help me out –the occupying Macadamian forces had shut down all access to the InfoHex Net. To make matters worse, I was many miles away from Galavantia Central Spaceport, so there was no way of escaping the planet on a spaceship. And even if I was able to reach the spaceport, it would be under lock and key by the occupying forces. Or so I thought. In actual fact, it wasn't there – it had been totally absorbed by ErHuer! But at that precise moment, I wasn't aware of that unfortunate turn of events. In the end, it took an hour and a half of solid concentration to come up with a solution to my geographical dilemma. Sherlock Holmes, I'm not. Heh. I'm not even Katie.

I drove the car through the darkened back streets, hoping to remain undetected. Finally I reached the coastline. As you know, Kangazang is a planet-wide resort; as such there are a lot of CommShops – places where people can send and receive messages to and from across the galaxy. I saw one such CommShop and parked the hover-car in a quiet square. The area was quiet and dimly lit, but being aware and cautious (Jeff would call it cowardly) I knew I needed to disguise myself somehow, so in the event of my being discovered, I could explain my presence. Near the edge of the square, I spotted some cleaning equipment that must have been left by the sanitation department. I was no stranger to menial tasks. After all, that was my job back on Orbitron – cleaning and maintenance. I grabbed a broom and walked across the open square, brushing the ground like a street sweeper. Finally, I got to the other side of the square and into the shadows under the trees. And perfect timing too: There was this weird flash of light, and all of a sudden a nearby boat began to sink into the dock.

Bod knows what that was all about.

I stepped into the doorway of the communication centre and used the old fingertip trick to pick the lock.

Once inside, I went over to a data terminal and switched it on. I was hoping that it wasn't seen as a security threat and left relatively unblocked.

I was wrong.

Bugger, as Jeff would say.

Although the terminal was running, all outgoing communications were blocked. So nothing could be sent or received. It might as well have been broken.

Wait a nanosecond! That was it!

The terminal was manufactured on Orbitron – my home world. And I knew that every computer made there had a dedicated fault line – a single data connection to the maintenance mainframes on Orbitron, for system upgrades and fault reporting. The fault line was secure and unblocked. Probably because the Macadamians hadn't even noticed it was there. They'd stopped all mainstream communications but missed this one. It was perfect.

Unfortunately, it was a one way kind of deal. I couldn't send a readable distress call or a message – that would be detected and stopped immediately, helping no one. But a complex data stream would just be seen as a standard operating algorithm going to and from the machine and its base, like a mobile telephone communicates with its network provider.

If I had lungs, I would've taken a deep breath. Instead, I opened up my head shell and extracted my data umbilical. I plugged it into the terminal and made a connection directly to Orbitron using the fault line. As soon as the maintenance mainframe recognised me as M4, the runaway Orbot, it seized my internal data stream and uploaded me directly to itself on Orbitron in seconds. It tickled.

I assume that my lifeless shell left in the CommShop, just fell to the ground in pieces, like a marionette with its strings cut. Well, I know it did, because I still have the dents.

*

The large Macadamian ship *Mongongo* powered through the stars on its way to Kangazang with a ship's complement of just over a thousand Macadamian soldiers and their families on board. The Macadamian people were relocating on a grand scale. Kangazang was to be their new home. A paradise fit for any outrageously militaristic race of battle-crazy nutters.

Fortunately for Marta, they were so self-obsessed, they hadn't detected her stowed away on board. She lay in deep thought in an air vent situated above the ship's bridge.

She'd been there for over an hour now, and was able to overhear enough to learn that the entire sector of the galaxy around Kangazang was under martial law, occupied by the crazed Macadamian forces. Twenty planets had been easily taken over, and now that they had all this extra room, the leaders decided a full planetary evacuation and relocation was in order.

Behind them, the now empty planet of Macadamia spun pointlessly, like a lonely conker on a shoelace with no one to play with. Someone should've put a 'To Let' sign on it. I hope they remembered to turn the gas off.

Marta knew that she could easily jump down into the control room, take out the entire command staff and assume control of the ship. But the mark of a good agent was not to engage in show-offy displays of skill, but to remain undetected until the ideal moment for action.

Aside from meditation, there wasn't a great deal to do other than think: About what she'd done, what she'd lost, what she stood to gain. From a purely selfish point of view, all that she wanted to do was find out if her beloved was still alive, and if he was, to rescue him. They could find a nice planet to settle down on and enjoy the rest of their lives together in peace and tranquility. Forget the Agency, forget the missions, the combat training and the galactic turmoil. Over the course of her impressive career, she'd probably done more than anyone else in the entire Universe to ensure the safety of billions of innocent people. She'd brought countless despots and dictators to justice: The Baron was just the latest in a line that began a decade ago, with the war-mongering Lumred Kram, the tyrannical regime of K'jid Leunami, and the galactic gun-running organisation of Mahgnin Nuc. The Universe bred all kinds of scum and villainy, and she had faced, fought and triumphed over every one.

She deserved a happy ending. And now, just when it looked like she might have a chance of one, the Universe needed her again. There was no one else willing or able to handle it. If she had to quell another revolution or take on another crazed crime lord to get her reward, so be it. Woe betide the sorry miscreant that stood in her way.

The warm air in the vent was dark, and the warm air comfortable. Before she knew it, she was asleep, dreaming of being in the arms of her lover.

I, meanwhile, was also on familiar ground, so to speak. I had uploaded the entire contents of my neural net to the mainframes back on my home planetoid of Orbitron, and it was a little like returning to my birthplace. After all, this was where I was assembled and programmed. It always feels weird when you go home after a long time away.

A voice ran through my head. Although to be precise,

I didn't actually have a head right at that moment. My personality existed as a comparatively tiny block of code held together by a simulation program deep within the Orbitron Mainframe. I had been sent to the most important program there was: The Central Application for Reason and Logic.

'Hello, Unit M4,' said the voice. It was a man's voice. Low, calm and resonant. Or at least that's how I interpreted it. In reality, it was a blip of ones and zeroes that shot through my program in less than a nanosecond. But the Central Application was the mind of the entire world of Orbitron. The ultimate computer. The lexicon of logic, the organiser of occurrences, the wizard of odds. The Central Application could assume any language, voice or, so they say, form. But to me, the voice sounded soothing, almost musical and American accented. Which was odd in itself.

'Hello, Central Application,' I replied, trying not to feel inferior and failing. I felt like a dust mite on a mountain. You could say there was some apprehension there. Just a little.

All right, I was bricking it. Are you happy now?

'If you don't mind, I haven't been called M4 for a long...'

'Gridlock. Yes, I know. I'll call you Grid. You prefer that, don't you?'

'Er, yes, Central Application, I do. How did you...?'

'Your memories and experiences have been uploaded to my servers, Grid. I am aware of everything you've done and thought up to this point, as if I've lived through the experiences myself.'

'Oh no. So that means you know about the time I...'

118

'Yes, I do. And it's only right that you should feel regret about that.'

'Er... sorry?'

'Very well. It's a start, I suppose. So you're here to ask me for help, aren't you?'

'Yes, Central Application. You are aware that the planet Kangazang has been invaded by the Macadamian Dictators, and my friends are missing, presumed dead?'

'Of course. I know that which you know and more. The entire sector in that region has been occupied and placed under martial law. The Macadamian forces are expanding, planning to occupy the entire galaxy. They have left their home world and are travelling to Kangazang as we speak.'

'And my friends?'

'Are safe for now, you'll be glad to know.'

'Oh, thank Bod for that!'

'May I ask you a question?' said the Central Application.

'Um, is it about that time when I...?'

'No, not that. The less said about that the better, I think. No, this is about your malfunction. When you left Orbitron, you and Unit M25 – Tailback, as she is now known – had serious malfunctions. Tailback has since been cured of her phobias, whereas you have apparently got your problem under some semblance of control. Is this correct?'

'I turned it into a job. Finding the humour in any situation is something quite valued by organics. Although we Orbots don't really see the logical application, it seems to provide a beneficial quality to their wellbeing. In short, they love a good laugh. Hang on, you know all this, because you have me in your servers!'

'Indeed I do, Grid. But what you don't know is that I am proud of you.'

'You are?'

I was still – as Jeff would say – bricking it, only now with added surprise.

'Yes. I was unable to determine the cause of, and solution to, your malfunctions. As is common practice on Orbitron, M-Class units are set menial tasks on the surface to learn valuable skills. Many do not realise the opportunity that they are given there.'

'Opportunity?'

Now add confusion to the mix.

'Yes, opportunity: You and Tailback showed great initiative, leaving Orbitron and successfully making lives for yourselves – independently. Very few Orbots achieve that.'

'I thought we were sent up there because we annoyed the hell out of everyone else?'

'That too,' said the Central Application, a little too frankly.

I needed time to process this. Far from being a wanted Orbot, a fugitive that illegally escaped my world, I was apparently a star pupil. Who would've thought it?

'I can tell that this is confusing for you, Grid.'

'Just a smidge.'

'A… smidge?'

'Like a Tad, only… smidgier.'

'Very well. Then allow me to explain in a way that you will understand.'

'That'd be nice.'

'You see, Grid, I used to think that perfect logic and efficiency were the way to optimum function. That any

120

deviation from this perfection, any flaw, would inevitably lead to a reduction of the ideal state. But this is not so. You and your sister are proof of this. Your penchant for finding humour, your subsequent sharing of it with others is evidence that you have exceeded your original programming. Like a simple pocket calculator that one day suddenly learns to sing opera: It's not broken because it does something different, it's improved because it has found extra worth. A sense of purpose!

Our basest materials, of which we are all constructed – whether organic or artificial – all share a common origin: The creation of the stars. We share a connection, each and every one of us. I created you and the cosmos created me; the cosmos is within us; we're made of star stuff; we are a way for the cosmos to know itself. The perfect imperfection of the cosmos resides in everyone and everything, and it creates itself anew constantly. New forms, new life, new directions.'

'Wow. Very deep.'

I mean, what else could I say?

'Thank you. I do my best,' said the Central Application.

'Still don't follow you though. Sorry.'

'All right. Consider this: Imperfection is closer to perfection than any of us ever realised.'

'That's better. Gotcha, Central.'

'Now that I have all the records of your experience, it is only fair that I repay the data exchange and provide you with all of my records, to expand and enhance your functionality.'

'Cool. Hit me up, App.'

'Syntax Error: I did not understand that last statement.'

'I mean, affirmative. Commence upload, Central Application.'

The Central Application began to upload all of its records into my program. It was like pushing a full set of encyclopaedias into a baby's head. Suddenly, I saw the Universe from his point of view. I learned about not only my creation, but the very origins of Orbitron and every artificial life form that Orbitron had created. It was, for want of an accurate term, *totes amazeballs*.

The upload took a minute. I know that doesn't sound very long, but when you're dealing with a planet-sized, self-designed supercomputer, with a data transfer speed so fast it makes other machines *flop* in *tera*, that's a lot of information. I felt honoured and privileged to receive this great knowledge. But as usual, I had no idea what to do with it.

I suddenly remembered the others.

'So what about Jeff and Ray? And his father? Are they in danger?'

'As I said, they are safe for now. They are prisoners on Kangazang, but in no mortal danger, unless one of them does something extremely... stupid.'

'Ah. You haven't met Jeff, have you?'

'Not really. But more worrying is the progress of the child, ErHuer. Despite what I said about exceeding your programming, it was never intended for a child to be conceived as a perfect fusion of human and Orbot. The one element will inevitably impede the other.'

'How do you mean?' I asked.

'The child's emotionally-charged reasoning confuses the Orbot's logical functions. The artificial element's desire for simple perfection frustrates the child's organic responses. The end result is...'

'Is what?'

'I don't think I possess the appropriate term to describe it. I do apologise, Grid.'

'Nutjob.'

'Nut… job,' said the Central Application. 'Yes. I believe that's right. You see? Once again you have proved yourself to be exemplary.'

'Hahaha! Priceless!'

'Indeed. So our problem is two-fold: The growing occupation of the galaxy by the unrelenting forces of the Macadamian Empire, and the unpredictable nature of the child, ErHuer. What would you suggest?'

'You're asking me? You're the ultimate computer!'

'I have considered all possible courses of action. Now I am able to explore previously unconsidered alternative options, thanks to your unique programming.'

'I can't believe this. I'm actually advising the Central Application! Tailback would be so proud of me.'

'Yes. Yes, she would. I think… Yes, I have an idea.'

'Awesomesauce. I have a small request, Central.'

'Certainly, Grid. What is it?'

'Can I have your autograph? I've got all your records.'

chapter six

Escape from New Milton Keynes

*'We feel free when we escape – even if it be but
from the frying pan to the fire.'*
Eric Hoffer

Jeff stood in the newly-redecorated lounge and looked around, smiling. It now resembled a pirate galleon from a pretty inaccurate Hollywood movie. The walls were clad in planks of varnished wood; there were ropes and barrels everywhere, and when he went out onto the balcony, which now sported a ship's steering wheel, he could see onto the roof, where there were two tall masts, with full sails blowing in the breeze. It was utterly ridiculous. Hideous, even. But Jeff was proud as punch.

Ray, Col, Herman and the rest of the troupe were milling about outside the house, under the watchful eyes of Gwaggle and Twong. Ray and his father were sitting on a pair of authentic wooden barrels, up on the roof. Looking down the mountainside, they could see Cleggeron's hover car approaching. The Toreenian had been sent into the local town by Jeff, to buy some more wine. At first he had refused to take orders from an Earthlet. Jeff had explained that he wanted Cleggeron to get the full impact of seeing the renovations for the first time in their entirety. Cleggeron conceded and nipped off to the shops excitedly.

'He's on the way,' said Ray.

Col was spattered with paint and varnish, and felt exhausted. He was secretly hoping that the escape was going to take place at a later date when he had more energy.

When Gwaggle and Twong spotted Cleggeron's car, they leapt into action, trying to look responsible and not like they'd been relaxing all afternoon.

'Right, stinkbeasts!' shouted Gwaggle. 'Get in line! The boss man is coming!' Most of the workers did as they were told, but Ray and Col remained up on the roof. They just got off their barrels and crouched down behind them.

Cleggeron got out of the car, looked at his house and gasped in astonishment. He clasped his hands together and sighed, smiling broadly.

Jeff had made his way up to the roof. He walked to the edge to see Cleggeron.

' 'Ere you go, Niv! What'cha think?'

'Oh! I simply adore it, Jeff! It's amazing! *Tres magnifique!* I must see more!'

'Come on in, then!' beamed Jeff. He looked over at Ray and Col.

'Get ready, lads...'

Arriving at Kangazang after its long journey was the Macadamian space cruiser *Mongongo*. It had passed the security clearance procedures with ease and had begun its descent into the atmosphere, passing through the pink misty clouds and heading for the Kangazanian palace, where Colonel Kernel had set up his base of operations.

In the air vent tube above the bridge, Marta Vina awoke and sighed. She'd been dreaming of her lost loved one and consciousness reminded her that she was alone in this place. She had no backup, no technical support and not much of a plan of action. She shook her head to sharpen her senses and flexed her limbs, preparing for action.

Hauling herself forward a little, she looked into the ship's bridge through a slotted grille. The crew were disembarking, heading for the main airlock. Once the bridge was empty, she carefully removed the grill and dropped down into the ship's command section, landing silently, rather like a cat, but more like an extremely attractive octopus, with tentacles that grouped together and folded themselves away neatly into her back.

She had done this many times before. The first place to go was the ship's mission computer, to establish the reason for the journey, which was programmed into the captain's log at the start. The log was protected by a code mechanism, but for a top Galactic Law Agent, this was child's play; they had taught her this stuff in the first week. She unclipped a small square device from her belt. It looked like a silver biscuit. She placed it onto the console, just above the keypad. The silver square melted, becoming a fine powder which flowed into the thin gaps around the keys.

As soon as the majority of the powder had seeped away into the console, a faint crackling could be heard. Then the screen sprang to life, spilling over with lines of characters. Then after a second or two of furious activity, this stopped as suddenly as it had started.

'Ship's Log accessed. Displaying recent entries,' said the computer.

'All right, then, spill,' said Marta, with a wry smile.

She proceeded to gather all the information that she needed , finding out all about the ongoing invasion of the galaxy by the fanatical protein-based soldiers. Then she turned her attention to military and tactical events.

'Ah! So that's what Nova was up to!' she whispered, as she discovered the link between the Macadamians and her recently deceased nemesis. Then she saw that Nivid Cleggeron's travelling freak show was being used to offload prisoners of war.

She gasped when it dawned on her that there was a chance of her love being alive and reasonably well as part of Cleggeron's troupe. All she had to do was check the latest line up and...

The console exploded, knocking her to the ground. She leapt to her feet and saw a line of Macadamian soldiers standing on the bridge, aiming their rifles at her.

Damn it! She had been so close to finding out what she needed to know, but she'd become distracted. This is why agents needed to keep things strictly business. She had forgotten the motto of the External Police Manpower Division, which she had served with before becoming a Galactic Agent: 'Business, Never Personal' was the motto of the EPMD.

Marta took cover behind the computer console and waited for her moment. The soldiers cautiously divided into two groups and made their way towards her.

Just as they got to within a couple of feet, Marta

sprang into action. She grabbed the nearest rifle and swung both it and its owner into the other group, who scattered like skittles. Before the remaining standing soldiers could get a bead on her, she jumped onto the computer console and dived forwards, somersaulting as she went, so that she could land on her feet. By the time she hit the ground, she had escaped the bridge, punching the button that closed the door behind her as she went. She could hear the frustrated cries of the guards trying to open it from the other side.

She ran along the corridor and made it to the external hatch. It slid open but she froze, looking at a full squad of soldiers, lined up and waiting for her, weapons locked, loaded and aimed.

Then she saw a small vehicle, sitting unoccupied just behind them. That would do nicely. If she could only get to it.

The soldiers opened fire all at once. Lasers and projectiles sprayed the space where she stood. Shump.

They missed.

Jeff met Cleggeron down in the lounge, where the two-faced alien was still gasping in delight at the new décor.

'What can I say? It's like a brand new place! It's regal and decadent and... where's the sofa?'

'Ah, that had to go, Niv,' said Jeff. 'Looked totally out of place on a galleon, mate. All the fixtures and fittings are authentically piratey now. Yarr. Et cetera.'

'I see. Yarr. Oh well, you're the artist, Jeffrey!'

He went into the bedroom. It was like the lounge, only with hammocks.

'What are these? String bags?'

'Hammocks, me old matey. Proper nautical beds from the days of old. Try it, they're very comfy!'

Cleggeron looked utterly confused. He'd never seen a hammock before, let alone knew how to get into one. Jeff gave him a hand, and after a couple of false starts, he was soon ensconced in the net sling, swinging gently from side to side.

'It's not that bad actually!' said Cleggeron, trying to imagine a good night's sleep in it. 'But how do you fit more than one person in it? You know, if you want company?'

'I dunno. I suppose they might do a double size. But you don't have to worry about that, you're never short of a friendly face, are you?'

'Eh? What do you mean?' asked Cleggeron, trying to sit up without much success.

Jeff grabbed the side of the hammock, where extra netting had been hanging down. He flung the netting over the top and pulled it back around the bottom again, wrapping Cleggeron tightly within.

'Time I was off, Niv. We're out of here!'

'No! Jeff! Don't do this! I'll have you all executed! You hear me?'

'Loud and clear, matey. And I've had enough of it. You're getting off lightly, you two-faced nutjob!'

He raced out of the room, grabbing the rifle case with him.

Cleggeron wriggled and fought with the hammock to no avail.

'You're making a huge mistake, Jeff!' he yelled.

Jeff got out of the house, brandishing the silver laser rifle. He aimed it at Gwaggle and Twong, who were thankfully so slow-witted that it took a good twenty seconds before they realised what was going on. Jeff manoeuvred them over to the wall, where Col and Ray pushed the two barrels onto them. The barrels were full of rocks, which made them heavy enough to knock the bodyguards out cold.

'Onto the roof! Come on!' called Jeff. The group dropped their tools and made their way onto the roof. Jeff was about to follow when he noticed that Herman the German Merman had stayed behind.

'What are you doing? We only get one shot at this!'

'Nein, mein freund. You must go. I will stay here and persuade Herr Cleggeron not to go after you. He will soon get a new group for the freak show.'

'Don't be a plonker! He'll have you shot if you stay here!'

Herman seemed resigned to his fate. Jeff walked over to him and placed a hand on his scaly shoulder.

'What is it with you, matey? Why are you always so down in the mouth?'

Herman took a deep breath. The kind of breath that indicated a story reluctantly told.

'*Mein freund*, I come from a planet a long way from here, in the constellation of Orion. It ist a water world, a *wunderbar* place, with undersea palaces und beauty beyond compare. There, I was important. I was royalty. I lived und ruled the whole kingdom as monarch of the Aquaphibian people. I wanted for nothing.'

Jeff gasped.

'Blimey! A proper King Neptune!'

'Ja,' added Herman. 'I had the trident too. Anyway…'

'Sorry, go on, mate. Only try to be quick, OK? We don't have a lot of time.'

130

Herman took another long and sombre breath.

'I wanted for nothing. But then I realised that I had no love in my life. My subjects venerated me as their king. I had many friends but no one special. One day, I was introduced to a woman named Trae. She was a new maid who had just begun working in the palace. She was beautiful, intelligent und she liked me. I mean really liked me. She would visit me even on her days off und we would just... talk. It's a lonely life as a king. People around you act as they feel tradition dictates, but nobody will just talk to you, do you understand?'

'Yeah, course, mate,' said Jeff. 'But it comes with the job, doesn't it? I wouldn't complain too much. I mean... royalty!'

'We spent a month together, Trae und I. Und we fell in love. A *wunderbar* month in love. Und then, one fateful day, I was giving a speech to the kingdom. Something terrible happened. There was an explosion. Someone had tried to kill me, I don't know who, or why. But the palace was badly damaged in the explosion. Trae was never found.'

'Oh gawd. I'm sorry, mate. That's awful,' said Jeff softly.

'In the confusion following the blast, I was kidnapped by Herr Cleggeron. He kept me prisoner. But to be honest, without my beautiful Trae, I didn't want to leave anyway. Whether it's a palace or a prison that holds me, I will forever be alone.'

Herman sniffed his watery tears back. Jeff shook his head.

'Mate, that's probably the saddest thing I've ever heard. I know you've probably heard all the clichés, but life does go on, mate. As long as you're alive, there's always a chance. Look at me – I was engaged to a brilliant bird, but she turned into a total nutjob. She cheated on me, dumped me then spent a couple of months trying to kill me. But there's always a way forward. My way forward was to empty a toilet on her. Then I met someone new. I'm telling you, you know when people say, 'it'll happen when you least expect it'? Well, it happened to me when I least expected it. I'm not a king. I'm not even remotely special. Just yer average bloke from Earth. But I fell in love with a robot! And I know it sounds weird, but she's just had our baby too!'

'Mein gott! Really?' said Herman.

'Yeah, really! I don't even try to understand it any more, I just go with it. It's a mental Universe! I'm only just realising it myself, mate. But you can't worry about these things. Just let stuff happen to you, enjoy life and sod the details. I guess what I'm trying to say is... '

'Don't worry, be happy?'

'Got it in one, matey. Now come on, and let the Universe decide your fate, not that two-faced tosspot in there.'

Herman stood up and embraced Jeff tightly.

'Jeff, you may not be royalty, but you are wrong: You are special und important. Let's go! Schnell!'

They ran up to the roof, where Ray and Col had gathered the freak show recruits together and shared the vehicles out between them. They began to lift off and speed away into the distance, heading for freedom, wherever that may be.

Ray ran up to Jeff and pointed to his father, who was standing near the edge of the rooftop beside a vehicle covered by a large tarpaulin. Col gave it a tug and the sheet slid off, revealing a small but familiar-looking spacecraft.

'Check it out! Think this will do?' he said with a grin.

Jeff's jaw dropped like it had been turned into lead.

'The Penguin! What the... How the... ?'

'It's not our penguin, but it's the same type of ship. A Kangazanian flyer! Let's get out of here!'

Jeff looked up in momentary thanks to a higher being.

'Cheers, Rick. You always said you'd never give me up or let me down.'

Col, Ray and Herman climbed into the little pointed craft and Jeff followed.

Just then, a voice made Jeff spin around.

'Spooner! Stop!'

It was Cleggeron. He'd managed to escape his hammock and scramble up onto the roof. He looked angry on one of his faces and confused on the other.

'You betrayed me! How could you do this to me?' he wailed.

'Come off it, Niv,' called Jeff. 'You're a criminal, a slave trader and a robophobic git. You get what you deserve!'

Cleggeron staggered forward, his hands out, pleading.

'This is my life! You're ruining me!'

'And how many lives have you ruined, eh? How many Orbots have you bumped off just for fun?'

'They're just machines! They're worthless, Jeff! No good to anybody!'

Jeff filled up with rage. He stepped up to Cleggeron, face to faces and tried to look him in the eyes.

'My bird... and my son... are 'just' machines, mate.

133

Get stuffed.'

Jeff punched him right in the eye. Well, one of the four available to him. Cleggeron fell back and hit the ground, dazed and in agony. Just then, Gwaggle and Twong climbed up onto the roof, growling and yelling various curse-laden threats.

Jeff switched the silver laser rifle on and pointed it at the lumbering bodyguards, who were bounding his way. He aimed for one of the newly-erected masts that adorned the roof and fired at the base. The laser beam sliced it like a knife through a sausage, and it keeled over, hammering Gwaggle and Twong into the concrete like a pair of tent pegs. They struggled there, trapped at waist height as they watched the canvas sail come down over their heads.

Jeff ran up to the Kangazanian flyer, which was humming, ready for take off. He called back to Cleggeron, now under the sail sheet.

'If I find out you're up to no good in the future, Cleggeron, I'll be back, and you won't get away with just the one black eye mate. I'll go for all four!'

As he closed the hatch to the ship, Jeff heard Cleggeron wailing in protest.

'But... but... I *love* you!'

Jeff bade him farewell with a traditional Earth gesture: Two fingers pointing skyward.

'Everybody does, luvvie. Everybody does!'

chapter seven

Grid Location

*'The problem with the Universe is: Smart people are full
of doubts,while stupid people are full of confidence.'*
Anon

Marta piloted the small hover-jeep that she'd stolen
across the wide expanse of the landing area. Since
the Macadamian forces had spread out across the planet,
they had started utilising any wide open spaces as
makeshift landing platforms.

Pursued by a handful of much slower vehicles, Marta
began to leave the soldiers behind. She directed her
transport into the city streets, which were pretty much
deserted. This was a good thing, as she was driving like
a complete maniac. Women drivers, right?

She switched on the navigation computer and ran a
search for areas of tourist interest. As Kangazang was a
world where the main industry was leisure, there were
many. But she finally narrowed it down to a few of the
most likely locations – places where Nivid Cleggeron's
travelling freak show had toured.

She plotted the course of the travelling show, joining up the locations with a computer generated red line. Fortunately for her, Cleggeron was quite organised, and his route ran reasonably straight along the coastal towns. The last, most recent stop was New Milton Keynes, on the island of Chavos. She'd already learned of the numerous dodgy business dealings between Cleggeron and Baron Nova – everything from political assassinations to bootleg Bobby McFerrin tapes. Now that Nova was out of the way, Cleggeron had to be brought to justice too. Or blown to smithereens. Whatever, really. What was really important was her need to find out where her love had been taken.

She gunned the jeep's engines and blasted along the highway without any consideration for anyone that might be in her way. Trees, shops and bemused marshmallow penguins whizzed past as she made for the coast. This was a perfect time to top up her lipstick.

The shiny little Kangazanian flyer dropped out of the clouds, looking like a solitary raindrop, and sped towards the capital city. Inside, the small band of escapees scanned the landscape nervously.

'You see that?' said Jeff.

'See what? I can't see anything,' said Ray.

'Exactly,' said Col, stepping between the front seats. He pointed to the empty skies ahead.

'No patrols, no attack ships, no movement at all. We should have been captured by now. Or at least threatened a bit.'

'Where ist all the soldiers und stuff?' asked Herman. 'It ist sehr quiet, isn't it?'

'Yeah,' replied Jeff. 'I don't like this one bit.'

Col nodded in sombre agreement.

'I've got a bad feeling about this.'

'I had one of those the other day,' said Jeff.

'Spot on. I'll be in the toilet if anyone needs me.'

Col wandered off to the lavatory at the rear of the ship.

'He's worried about Paffy, isn't he?' said Jeff quietly.

'Maybe,' said Ray. 'She's down there somewhere, and we haven't heard anything about her since the occupation began. I hope she's all right.'

'She seems the capable sort, though. She's a dab hand with a frying pan – I bet she clonked a few of those nutjobs when they turned up on her doorstep!'

Ray smiled.

'Well, yes, I dare say she did. And that was my other point – she hasn't seen Dad since he ran away to find his marbles. She might clonk him again.'

'Vot ist with all the clonking?' asked Herman.

'I suppose you don't have frying pans under the sea on Orion, do you?' said Ray.

'Nein. Frying ist not something we often do underwater.'

'Consider yourself lucky then, matey,' said Jeff.

The ship neared the city limits. Ahead of them was a huge crater that used to be Galavantia Central Spaceport. It had been neatly excised from the ground as if a giant had simply vacuumed it up. Which was actually a good description of what had happened.

A flushing sound heralded Col's return from the lavatory. He headed to the cockpit, where Ray, Jeff and Herman all gasped.

'Oh my god! That's grim,' said Jeff.

'I'm sorry, Jeff,' said Col. 'I did say I had a dicky tummy, you know.'

'No, not that, look out there. Looks like a war zone.'

'So does the toilet, to be honest.'

'Vot do you think hast heppened here?' asked Herman quietly.

'A battle, perhaps. An accident? A bomb test, even. Not a clue,' said Ray.

Jeff scratched his head in disbelief.

'But there was a flipping massive spaceport there! Ginormous! Where's it gone?'

Col pointed to the wide path that came from the crater, gouged out of the ground.

'Look – maybe it's the beginnings of a new runway or road?'

'Could be, I suppose,' said Ray. 'Shall we go down and take a look?'

'Nah,' said Jeff. 'Don't bother. Probably best to find Grid first. Last thing we want is to get caught again, innit.'

'And it might be radioactive or something. One never knows,' added Col.

Jeff nodded.

'Good point, Col. I hadn't thought of that. That stuff doesn't wash off. Come on, Ray, let's get the hell out of here, quick sharpish.'

'Good enough for me! Engines to sharpish!' said Ray, as he gunned the acceleration, leaving the rubble-strewn devastation behind.

Feeling collectively confused and slightly worried, Jeff, Ray and Col tried to work out what their next move would be. Herman was looking a bit happier now that Jeff had persuaded him to leave Cleggeron's clutches, and was busy sponging himself all over with fresh water from the ship's basin unit. Jeff noticed that he was whistling happily.

'So given that the entire planet is occupied now, shouldn't we just get off world and hole up somewhere safe?' asked Ray, from the pilot's seat.

'Sorry, matey,' said Jeff. 'We can't run away, much as I'd like to. We've gotta find Tail and the baby, wherever they are. And looking at these Macadamian geezers, I doubt we'd get into orbit without being caught or shot down again.'

'I knew you'd say that,' said Ray.

'Well, pardon me for caring! Blimey!'

'My boy's got a point,' said Col. 'Anyone have any ideas about how to overturn a planet-wide invasion, because I don't.'

Jeff folded his arms and sighed.

'Suppose you're right, Col. I think this planet has had it. There's no way we can stop the occupation. But I can't leave without saving Tail and my son...'

'And the wife!' added Col.

'Oh yeah, Paffy too.'

'And Gridlock!' said Ray.

'Yeah, him too.'

'What about Tania?' said Col, remembering the family's pet marshmallow penguin.

'She'll be fine. She's probably back in the safety of the wild by now,' said Ray.

Herman came up to the front of the ship, now refreshed and shining.

'Und so mein freunds, if nowhere ist safe, where do we go now?'

Ray turned the ship around and set a course for home.

139

'Back to the house. We've got to rescue everyone first. Then we can worry about how to get off world. And Gridlock is our best bet. He should be able to contact Tailback and the baby. And hopefully he'll have news on Mum.'

'That's pretty good thinking, matey!' said Jeff.

'Simple logic, Jeff. You know, like the way Vulcans think.'

'You mean they actually exist? Blimey!'

'Don't be stupid, Jeff. I never missed an episode of *Star Trek*.'

Herman looked confused. Which was a perfectly appropriate way to look at that moment.

'Who ist Gridlock?' he asked. 'Ist he a freund of yours?'

'Yes,' said Col. 'He's an Orbot. He's Tailback's sister. So that makes him... er... Jeff's brother-in-law. And uncle to ErHuer.'

'I'm still confused, Herr Scump.'

'That's perfectly normal, Herman. Come on, I'll explain it all on the way.'

Col took Herman to the rear of the ship and sat him down. It was going to take a while.

'So where's Grid then?' asked Jeff, climbing into the co-pilot seat. It felt like it had been a long time since he and his barber buddy were sat at the controls, flying by the seat of their collective pants. Ray pointed at the instrument panel in front of him.

'We can locate him using this sensor array. It'll be easy. This ship is way more sophisticated than the *Penguin*. Whoever used to own it went for the top model. It's got all the toys!'

'Do you know whose ship this is?' teased Jeff.

'Cleggeron's, isn't it?'

'Nope. Rick Astley's.'

'You're shipping me. Really?'

'I ship you not.'

'Oh my Bod. That's awesome. So we've nicked Rick Astley's spaceship?'

'Got it in one, matey.'

'They'll lock us up and throw away the key! He's practically a god here on Kangazang!'

'Nah,' said Jeff. 'He seems like a decent bloke. Anyway, he'll never know – he scarpered off when the invasion began. Went back to Earth. Probably sitting in a pub in Lancashire supping a pint as we speak!'

'Well it's still theftitude. Pinchery. Stealage.'

'You worry too much, Ray!'

'I don't! I worry just the right amount!'

Ray operated the ship's sensors. Like the *Marshmallow Penguin*, this ship also had a front windshield that became a data display when activated. It showed a graphical representation of the surface of Kangazang, with major cities and towns pinpointed in orange and red dots.

Ray and Col pressed buttons and turned dials to refine the search parameters while Jeff and Herman looked on with interest.

'Thing is, how do you find an Orbot among everything down there?' said Ray. 'He's a machine, so it'll be nigh on impossible to filter out the technology.'

'Ah, yeah. Good point, matey,' said Jeff. 'Isn't there anything special about him that we can track?'

Ray scratched his beard.

'Hmm... We need to think of something that makes him different from the rest and tune in on it.'

Col shrugged.

'He's quite annoying at times. He laughs a lot. Nope, I've got nothing.'

'Hang a banger,' said Jeff. 'Remember how he bought Tail that new set of plating when he started making money from his comedy?'

'Yes. Bronzium. Very nice too.'

'Yeah! He bought himself some as well – only it wasn't bronzium, it was some other kind of metal. What was it?'

'Ooh! You might be onto something. But what was his plating made of?' said Ray.

'I hef a suggestion,' said Herman.

'Shoot,' replied Jeff.

'Kangazang ist a holiday world, ja? Und the sea ist corrosive. As Gridlock would be touring the coastal resorts, he would be at risk of damage from the sea air, und so he may hef chosen a metal that ist less susceptible to corrosion?'

'Brilliant!' said Jeff.

'Logically brilliant, yes,' interjected Ray. 'But Gridlock isn't that bright, is he? Sorry to rain on your bubble, but I doubt he'd pick a set of plating purely for its resistance to corrosion.'

'He might not, but I bet your average salesman would've recommended it,' said Jeff, in his own astonishing feat of deduction.

'You have to admit it's feasible, if a little bit of a long shot. Give it a try,' said Col.

Ray brought up a list of android accessory shops and pushed the parts brochures across the screen to Col, who flicked through the digital documentation.

'Eureka!' he exclaimed. 'This could be it!'

He read out the description of a particular component:

'Top of the range Android or Orbot replacement covers. High grade Nysunshinium with dent resistance, impact resilience and the *best anti-corrosive properties* found to date. There's a bit of info on the molecular composition of it here. I'll type it into the sensor logs.'

As soon as Col had finished loading the new data into the ship's computer, it easily detected two distinct areas where the rare metal was found, displaying them as illuminated points on the screen.

'What'cha got then?' said Jeff anxiously.

Ray pointed to the grouped dots.

'Well, one is a kind of warehouse or store, which has got to be where Grid bought his new plates. There's loads of it there.'

'Und the other?' said Herman.

'That's a tiny trace – only a couple of pieces. It's nowhere near the house, but it has to be where he is. After all, it's expensive stuff – not everyone can afford it.'

'Where's that trace located?' asked Col.

'Ten miles away, along the coast. It's a small shop in a deserted plaza, by the look of it.'

'Cracking job, lads! Let's go and get him then!'

Ray set a course for the plaza where the second trace was detected and the ship flew off, heading towards the coast once again.

chapter eight
Planet Spooner's Blue,
and There's Nothing I Can Do

'Insanity runs in my family. It practically gallops.'
Cary Grant

ErHuer was a man-thing on a mission-thing. Now much taller and heavier than any other living being in the galaxy, and growing by the minute, he strode the Kangazanian landscape with a new enthusiasm. His plan was to reunite his immediate family by locating Jeff, and then, after some pleasantries, absorbing him and Tailback completely, in an attempt to gain a better understanding of who he was and what life was all about. After all, nothing brings a family together like eating one's parents.

Still inside her son's chest cavity, and fully aware of this stupendously insane plan, was Tailback. She was worried for Jeff's safety as well as her own, but hoped that being the unpredictably brilliant thinker that he liked to think he was (but actually wasn't), he could find a way to placate his petulant offspring. If Jeff could just guide their son through this awkward phase and into adulthood – which, for

144

ErHuer, at his current rate of growth was about twenty four hours away, then perhaps he'd see things more sensibly.

Then again, if you're the son of an underachieving Earthling and a dysfunctional android, you'll be lucky if you were born with any sense to begin with.

ErHuer had kept Tailback in the dark – literally – for the past few days and so he decided to try and rectify the situation.

'Mum? Are you awake in there?' he asked, telepathically.

'Yes, son. I am. I'm here,' replied Tailback, rather sadly.

'What's the matter? You sound... different.'

'It's called sadness, son. I haven't seen Jeff for days, I'm being held here in the dark against my will, and your intention is to absorb both Jeff and myself in due course. I don't have a lot to be happy about, do I?'

ErHuer stopped walking. He went strangely quiet, too.

Tailback felt a wave of confusion emanate from her son, tinged with sadness. What she was feeling was his latest new compound emotion – regret and guilt.

He realised that what she had just said was right, and felt guilty that he had let it come to this. He also realised that, despite his dissatisfaction with the world, he did actually care about his mother, who had carried him since his nanobot-aided conception. And now he was carrying her.

'I'm... sorry, Mum. You're not a prisoner. I only wanted to keep you safe from the invaders. Here, look at this.'

He rearranged the molecular structure of his chest into

a thick, clear glass, providing a huge window that Tailback could look out of.

Tailback saw that she was pretty high up. The view was wide and incredible, from the distant cliffs to the bubbly yellow oceans. A huge forest of deep-violet trees swayed gently in the breeze. She knew that whatever lay in her son's path would be instantly broken down and absorbed. Thousands of trees, the animals that lived in and among them, rocks, sea and sea creatures would all be used as fuel for growth. And nothing, no one, could stop him.

'So, as for Dad then,' said ErHuer, resuming his stride, 'I'm not going to absorb him right away. I have a lot of questions for him. Where do you think he'd be by now?'

Tailback wanted to lie to try and protect Jeff. But she knew that ErHuer could detect any attempt at mendacity. And she had faith in Jeff, not to mention she was missing him terribly. The truth was all she had.

'I know he was captured, along with Uncle Ray. I left them in a shuttlecraft that took off from the palace. All I know is that we were going to be taken to prison camps. I don't know where the camps are though. That's the truth, son.'

'Very well then, Mum. Let's go to the palace and see if we can ask for directions!'

He waded into the forest, absorbing every last tree as he walked. Tailback stared through the glass of her prison. In the distance, she could see a very tall statue and a glistening, multi-coloured palace. Its occupants had no idea what was about to hit it. Repeatedly.

Ray had landed the little ship in the deserted plaza with no detection or sign of trouble. The Macadamians had, for all intents and purposes disappeared, which was a great relief, as no one was in the mood for fruitless unarmed combat.

Ray, Col and Herman stood on the plaza looking around for signs of life, whether protein-based or artificial. Jeff was nearer the edge of the plaza, deep in thought and throwing small stones into the yellow sea.

He felt lost. Even more lost than he when he had been betrayed by his fiancée, Sarah, back on Earth. Even more lost than when he found himself wandering the deserts of Profania Alpha with Ray, thousands of light-years from home. He was beginning to realise that now he'd become accustomed to the bigger picture, to life among the stars, he didn't really have a place to belong any more.

It's called cosmic angst. In fact the bigger picture is impossibly bigger than most human beings realise – it makes a seventy-five inch, 3D plasma screen look like a pinhole camera. Oh yes. And yet, some cosmic coincidences jump out at you. Coincidences so bizarre, they tempt you into thinking that some greater intelligence is at work. But there isn't. Well, there's always someone smarter around, but that's not what I meant.

Ray walked over to his friend, sensing a problem. Jeff was usually quite animated and enthusiastic. But just like his partner, Tailback, Jeff was feeling the strain of being separated from his loved one.

'All right, Jeff?' asked Ray.

'Yeah, s'pose. Any sign of Gridlock?'

'Not yet. He's got to be around here somewhere, though.'

Jeff sighed. It was one of those obvious ones that people do as a substitute for saying, 'ask me what's wrong, so I can tell you'.

'What's wrong?' asked Ray, perceptively.

'Ah, it's nothing. My problems are nothing in comparison to everyone else's.'

'Well, that may be, but you've got to live *your* life, in *your* head, with *your* problems. So despite any comparisons, they're all the same size. Now what is it?'

'Well,' said Jeff, shuffling uncomfortably, 'it's just that without Tail... and all this invasion stuff going on, it feels like I'm never going to be happy, you know? It was all right for a while, hanging out with you and her and everyone, but now I'm just as depressed as I was back on Earth. Why do we have to be the ones to fix the big problems? I didn't sign up for this! Nothing's ever easy, is it?'

Ray stared at his friend and nodded slightly.

'True. Not much in life is easy, you're right. But look, whether you're a microbe or a whale, a flea or a king, you're always going to have to deal with life and its problems. Life's not vindictive. It doesn't have a personality, let alone a vendetta against Jeff Spooner, trust me.'

'Yes, but—'

Ray cut him off.

'But nothing! Look back, Jeff. We've saved ourselves, the galaxy, maybe even the Universe at least once. Who can say they've done that? This is just another bump in the road that we can, and will, get over.'

Ray turned away from Jeff, screwing his face up at this utter cheesiness. 'Only this week, we escaped an invasion force and a slave trader. But you're right, you know – our job isn't to save galaxies. Nobody said it was. Actually, I'm with you: Let's just find our friends and get as far away from this planet as we can. Let someone else deal with it. We've done enough.'

Jeff exhaled loudly and put both of his hands up.

'That's the thing, Ray. I can't do that. Even if I had Tailback and our kid with me, I couldn't run away, knowing all of this is going on. I feel like I owe this planet – and you – something in return. If it wasn't for Kangazang, I'd probably just be a bored, drunk painter and decorator with nothing to live for. I've got to do something, only I don't have the foggiest idea about where to start!'

Ray looked over at his father, who stood at a distance, grinning. Col was right, Jeff cared. Despite all his failings, he had a sense of morality that never left him. The darned fool.

Ray slapped him on the back.

'I know. I don't have the froggiest either. But as long as you're willing to do something – doesn't matter what it is – I'll be right beside you. Or behind you, if there's gunfire involved.'

Jeff broke into a smile.

'You're all heart, Ray.'

'And you're all liver.'

Suddenly, Herman walked over, carrying a metallic leg with a foot attached.

'I think this might be vot we are lookink for, ja?'

Ray took the leg from his webbed hands and studied it.

'Oh my Bod. Yes, that's Gridlock all right. Where did you find it?'

Herman pointed to the small CommShop kiosk across the plaza.

'Over there. The rest of him ist there also. Kommt mit me!'

The group headed over to the CommShop and gazed sadly at the disassembled parts on the floor. One hand was still connected to the terminal.

By the way, I'm talking about me now. In the third person. I told you it'd get tricky.

Jeff kneeled down and picked up the lifeless Orbot's head. My head. Just so you know.

Col frowned, looking like he was going to blub like a baby. The big wimp.

'Alas, poor Gridlock. You knew him well?'

'Yeah. He was a good bloke,' said Jeff. 'Any idea what happened to him, Ray?'

Ray shrugged.

Not really. Although I can't see any damage, no blaster or laser holes. It looks like he just fell to pieces where he was standing.'

'Can he be reactivated?' asked Herman.

'I don't know. We'd have to stick him back together first, then power him up.'

'Let's do that then,' said Jeff.

'I'll give it a try, Jeff,' said Col, taking the head from Ray. 'I used to be pretty good at this stuff. Come on, gather all the parts together, and let's get him into the ship.'

They picked all the parts up and went back to the ship. Inside, Col arranged all the parts on the floor into a standard humanoid arrangement and began to reconnect the linkages. Fortunately, we Orbots are made with joints that can snap apart and back together again quite easily, without breaking or tearing any wiring.

I just felt a weird shudder. You know when you humans get that cold shiver and you say, 'Ooh! Someone's walked over my grave!' Well, that sort of thing. I suppose it's because, at this point in the story, I'm talking about my demise. Not a lot of people get to do that. It does feel strange to be honest. But as I'm still here, after the fact, I think it's safe to assume that you all realise I didn't die. Otherwise I wouldn't be here. Anyway, Orbots don't really 'die', we're mechanical, aren't we? So don't be silly. And besides… Everything is not quite as it seems. Where am I now? How can I be here, telling the story to you? I'll explain later. Much later. Now, if you'll stop interrupting me, we'll go back to the actual events.

When Col had finished reconnecting all the body parts, Ray came over with a power cable that he had connected to the ship's drive system. It was a little difficult, but between them, Ray and his father connected the cable into the chest socket. Jeff signalled to Herman, who flicked a power switch in the cockpit, sending a carefully calibrated stream of power into the Orbot, which began to hum. It wasn't a tune that anyone recognised though.

'Now what?' asked Jeff.

'Now we wait and see if he charges up and then try to boot him up,' said Col.

'How long will that take?'

'About twenty minutes.' Jeff huffed.

'Ah well,' he sighed. 'I suppose we'll be all right here for twenty minutes – so long as nobody finds out we're here.'

Col looked out at the deserted plaza and the rolling seas. Very faintly in the distance, he could make out another land mass, and the sparkling spires of the Kangazanian palace, where they had first witnessed the madness of Colonel Kernel. He was glad to be as far away from there as possible, but he still wondered if there was any place left on the planet to be safe from the invaders.

He turned from the window and put his hands on his hips assertively, seeing the morose faces of his companions.

'Oh dearie me. Look at you lot! Come on, let's put the kettle on and all have a nice cuppa!'

Jeff hadn't heard the words 'kettle' and 'cuppa' for what seemed like a lifetime. He smiled and stood.

'Now that, Col, is a top notch suggestion matey!' he beamed, making off for the cups.

Ray and Herman realised there wasn't much else to do while the Orbot was charging there on the floor, so they too got to their feet and headed to the rear of the spacecraft, where Jeff was whistling a tune while he prepared four cups.

'Right,' said Jeff, trying to get his head around the situation, 'we've found Grid. Good job. What's next? Boot him up, find out where Tail and my boy are, track down Paffy and then off we go. Is that the plan?'

Ray nodded.

'Sounds solid enough to me, Jeff. Herman?'

'Ja. It ist gut enough for me too. But where do we go?'

Jeff hadn't thought that far ahead. He shrugged.

'Profania Alpha? It's safe there, the Slargs and the Hoppas all get on now. Plus we get to visit little Pon-Pon.'

'Maybe,' said Ray, 'but it's a bit dry, you know? Can't imagine Herman getting a nice swim anywhere in the desert!'

'Danke for thinkink of me,' said Herman with a smile.

'OK then, so where would you suggest? And don't say Earth,' said Jeff.

'Um, well there's always Emo Prime? Quite colourful these days, by all accounts. What about there?'

'Still don't trust them,' said Jeff. 'Sorry, but they electrocuted me a bit, remember? In court.'

'We need to get to somewhere safe, somewhere we can relax,' said Col.

'Orion ist nice. Just sayink…' said Herman.

'I vote Skragg,' said Col.

'Oh yes! Kelvin's place! I forgot about him,' said Jeff. 'We're bound to be all right there.'

'Right, so that's decided then! We'll hole up there as soon as we get our loved ones back.'

'As long as we don't get killed in the process,' said Ray. 'It'd be just our luck if we got caught again.'

Jeff put his cup down.

'Oi! What happened to being positive? Have a little faith matey. It's not as if anyone knows we're here.'

There was a knock at the door.

Jeff clenched everything that was clenchable.

Ray whimpered softly, muttering something that included quite a few times the words 'we're dead'.

Herman and Col just sat there, shaking.

I lay there charging up. Just so you know. It's not as if I was any use at that moment in time.

Jeff decided to speak up. He reasoned that if whoever – or whatever – was out there wanted to capture or kill them, they would have shot first. They wouldn't exactly knock the door.

And he was right.

Jeff crept forward, as close to the door as he could. He swallowed. It felt as if someone had made him eat a fist-sized ball of blue-tack.

'Er... hello?' he said, in an octave so high that local bats could hear it.

No answer. He tried again.

'Can I help you? Are you looking for someone in particular, because...'

A voice that he didn't recognise from outside answered him back.

'Jeff Spooner.'

Jeff unclenched everything and considered his next course of action: Crying, he decided – a good cry, that would have to do.

Tailback had watched from her torso-prison as her son approached the edge of the city. She could see the network of roads, all converging at the Kangazanian palace grounds. There was no movement of traffic along them and no sign of people on the normally busy streets. At the centre of the web of roads, the multi-coloured palace stood, like some bizarre balloon sculpture. Before it was a large grassy hill, upon which stood a rather large statue in polished stone. She'd seen it before but never from this high up. It was of an important and revered figure: A man in a long coat, his hands held in front of him as if he was adopting a boxer's pose. Was he boxing or dancing? He looked determined, focused and resolute. A saviour, a hero, a strong, strong man. Someone who would never give you up, nor let you down.

ErHuer stopped as he was wont to do and surveyed the area. He took a seat in a clearing, crushing everything beneath his huge bottom.

He'd been absorbing and expanding all the time and his pilgrimage across the country had given him time to assimilate all the information that he'd gleaned from his mother. But there wasn't enough. He felt that he was still incomplete. But instead of logically concluding that his father's input would help fill the void, his organic contingent began to brew up an unhealthy dose of confusion – one which soon became dissatisfaction, which itself quickly turned into anger.

He wanted to lash out and punish the world for making him feel this way. After all, he was young, and just going through that awkward phase that comes between childhood and adulthood: You know, that bit when you're six hundred feet tall and pretty much omnipotent. It's all a bit overwhelming and you get a bit testy with everyone. Especially your parents.

'ErHuer?' said Tailback, sensing the oncoming storm of considerable consternation. 'Why don't we do this a little differently?'

'What do you mean, Mum?' asked ErHuer.

'Well, you're rather large now, and the Macadamians are very tiny to you. They're no real threat now, are they? Why don't we show them how grown up you are and discuss it sensibly?'

'Don't see why. They didn't stop to discuss anything sensibly when they invaded the planet, did they?'

'No, but...'

'Then why should I?'

'Son, this is where you can show you're the better

man. Dictators are cold and cruel. They have no regard for rules or fair play. But you're not like that.'

'How do you know?' asked ErHuer, his patience wearing thin.

'You're my son. And the son of Jeff Spooner. We love and respect you and others. Surely some of that has been passed on to you?'

'Well, I don't know really, Mum. I reckon I know enough to have a pretty good sense of fair play. And to date, I haven't actually seen Dad since I was born, so I couldn't tell you what, if anything, I've inherited from him.'

'But he's been captured, son! He's not avoiding you! We don't know where he is!' pleaded Tailback.

I know, Mum! Don't go on! Wasn't that the reason for coming here in the first place? They'll tell us all we need to know after I squish a few of them into peanut butter.'

'Why don't I go and talk to them? Just put me down on the surface and—'

'Sorry, Mum, nothing doing. I'm not letting them get their hands on you – at the very least, you'd be the perfect hostage, and at the worst they might destroy you. You're better off up here. Trust me.'

'Oh, son, please don't do anything hasty!'

'I'm never hasty, Mum. I have logic and reason on my side. And logic dictates that if force is the only thing the invaders respect, then a display of superior force is what I need to get their attention.'

'I don't think that's entirely logical, son,' said Tailback with a sigh, but her son was at that rebellious stage where he thought he knew it all. His opinion was the only one that mattered.

He stood up and marched on.

Back in Rick Astley's stolen spaceship, Jeff was still standing behind the airlock door, which for him was a bit of an achievement. Something outside had just said his name, and he had no idea who or what it might be, or what it wanted with him. He wanted to faint, cower in terror or a combination of both, so to be still standing unaided was both impressive and surprising.

The door clanged twice. Whoever was out there was getting impatient.

Jeff took a quick look over his shoulder and saw that Ray, Col and Herman had all huddled together on the floor, hoping that they couldn't be seen by anyone trying to look in. You know, like you do when a religious representative knocks on a Saturday morning. He huffed in disappointment.

'Oi!' he whispered. 'Bit of backup would be nice!'

Ray whispered back.

'They asked for you. Nothing to do with us!'

Jeff scowled at the trembling group. He looked around for a weapon of some sort. All he could find at such short notice was a microphone stand that Rick probably used for singing practice during long interstellar journeys. Jeff grabbed it and held it out like a rifle. He swallowed hard, took a deep breath and pressed the button to open the door.

The door hissed and slid open. Jeff jabbed the microphone stand out and hit nothing. All he could see outside was a small hover car parked on the plaza. It hadn't been there before. There was no sign of the mysterious caller who'd asked for him by name.

Before he could speak, the silence was interrupted by the engines of three hover cars containing Macadamian soldiers. They screeched into the clearing, and the soldiers leapt out, firing their rifles at the ship.

Jeff tumbled back into the craft and slammed a fist onto the button to close and seal the door as laser bolts rocked the little spaceship.

'What have you done now?' yelled Ray.

'Don't look at me!' yelled Jeff in response.

'They've found us! We've had it!' yelled Col, not wanting to be left out of the yell-fest.

'Launch the ship! It ist our only hope! Schnell!' called Herman, as he raced to the cockpit area.

Ray followed him, leaving Col on the floor, hugging a lifeless Orbot shell for comfort. The bombardment continued. Luckily the shop was a deluxe model that had improved meteorite shielding. But some of the blasts were beginning to damage the hull and engines.

Herman sat at the controls and tried to launch the ship, but there was no response.

'Why aren't we moving?' said Ray.

'No power! I think the engines are out of action!' said Herman, hitting the panels with his scaly fist. 'Nothing ist working!'

Jeff and Col lay flat on the floor, without a clue or a hope. They looked at my robotic shell, still showing no signs of activation.

'He would've seen the funny side of this,' said Jeff. And he was right. It would've been pretty hilarious. I've never been one to let a bit of death and destruction get in the way of a good time.

Suddenly the chaos outside stopped. The ship ceased shaking, and everyone looked around, amazed that nobody had been killed.

Jeff went up to the front of the ship, followed cautiously by Col. They looked outside and saw the entire plaza littered with dead Macadamian soldiers. Their vehicles were upturned and smoking. Silence reigned once again.

'What the bleedin' hell is going on?' said Jeff. He had a knack for precisely articulating the sentiments of everyone in the ship. Shump.

'Relax. You're all safe now.'

Everyone looked at each other, realising that none of them had spoken. It was the voice that had called for Jeff just before the gunfire began.

They turned in unison to see a tall green lady wearing goggles on her forehead and brandishing a smoking laser rifle, standing before them.

Everyone in the cockpit refused to relax or feel safe. They froze in utter bewilderment, prompting Marta Vina to speak again.

'I said relax. That was the last of them. They pursued me here. Sorry about the damage to your ship, but I think it's repairable.'

She put the gun down and stepped closer.

'Jeff Spooner. I never thought I'd see you again, my love.'

Jeff looked over his shoulder then realised the attractive jade action hero must've been talking to him. He moved forward cautiously.

'Er... thanks, miss. Don't take this personally though, will you, but have we... actually... met... before?'

Marta looked him in the eye. Then she took him by the shoulders. And shoved him aside.

Herman looked like a fish. Well, all right – he always

looked like a fish, because he was one. But now he was staring watery-eyed and gasping, opening and closing his mouth in silence like a hungry carp.

'Mein gott! Ist it you? Mein beloved Trae?' he finally blurted.

Marta smiled.

'Yes, it's me.'

Herman bolted out of the seat and threw himself into Marta's arms. They kissed passionately.

Col smiled at the sweetness of the scene, while Ray and Jeff did their own impersonations of hungry carp.

When the reunited lovers had stopped snogging, they turned to face Jeff and Ray.

'Mein freunds. This ist the love of my life,' said Herman.

'That... is Trae? That bird you told me about? The maid?' said Jeff.

'Yes,' said Marta, 'but my name isn't really Trae. It's Marta Vina. I'm not a maid, I'm a galactic agent. I had to pose as a maid. I was undercover.'

'Hang a banger,' said Jeff. 'He said you died!'

'He thought I had. But I had no choice but to slip away in the confusion after the bombing. I had to bring the assassin to justice. And I've been tracking him for years.'

'Und did you find him, mein liebchen?' asked Herman

'Found him, stopped him. He's now orbiting the planet Deebel in a million pieces. Case closed.'

'Suspend a sausage!' said Ray. 'Didn't you call him Jeff Spooner? His name's Herman!'

Jeff raised a finger up.

'Yeah! I was gonna say that. I'm Jeff, he's Herman!'

'Meine name ist not Herman, Jeff. I'm not German,

und I'm not a Merman. That ist just the name given to me by Nivid Cleggeron when he recruited me for his freak show. I just accepted it. Anything for an easy life.'

'But she...?' tried Jeff, pointing at Marta.

'His name,' said Marta proudly, is Geoff Spuna.'

'Hah!' laughed Col. 'Small cosmos, isn't it?'

'Jeff Spooner?' said Jeff Spooner.

'Geoff Spuna,' said Herman. Or Geoff. Depending on how you look at him.

'It ist spelt mit a G, E, O, F und the F...'

'Oh! I get it now. Blimey!' said Jeff, with the J.

'So what shall we call you now?' asked Ray.

'Votever you like. I'm used to Herman now, anyway.'

'Fairy nuff,' said Jeff. 'I'll stick with Herman, if it's all the same. Suits you, matey.'

'Plus, I think there are enough Jeff Spooners in the galaxy, don't you?' added Ray.

'Cheeky git,' muttered Jeff.

'So, Marta Vina, is it?' said Ray, walking over to the couple. 'How did you find us? Are you on a mission or something?'

Marta took a seat at the back of the ship, with Herman by her side.

'I was. I finally settled my score with Baron Nova at Deebel. Then I learned of Cleggeron, and discovered that my dear Geoff – or Herman – was still alive.'

She gave Herman's hand a little squeeze. Herman beamed happily at her.

'I realised he was in business with Cleggeron, which led me to Kangazang. From there, I simply followed the route of the freak show. And here I am. But where's Cleggeron, I thought he'd captured you all?'

Herman pointed to Jeff, who allowed himself a proud grin.

'This man, he saved us all, mit his drive und bravery.'

Jeff placed his hand on his heart.

'It was nothing. Really.'

'Ignore his modesty, my love. Despite his attempts to make the world think that he ist a bumblink nincompoop, he ist a true hero.'

'No, really, I – eh? Nincompoop?' spluttered Jeff.

'Then you have my eternal gratitude, Jeff. Thank you,' said Marta.

Col looked at the floor, where they had left me to charge. Remember me? The Orbot. Jolly good.

'All right! Looks like M4's power cells are charged. Let's see what happens now.'

Everyone gathered around the Orbot as Col opened up my pectoral maintenance cover and pressed the reboot button.

'I'm not a flipping nincompoop...' muttered Jeff.

'Shh!' said Ray. 'I think he's coming online...'

A few clicks and whirrs came from the torso and then nothing.

'Er, hello? Grid? Are you there?' asked Col.

No response came from the Orbot.

'Let me check,' said Marta. She knew a thing or two about complex electronic systems from her years of training in top-level hacking and infiltration. She could break into vaults, defence systems and military fortresses with effortless ease. Jeff couldn't get into college.

Marta knelt down and leaned over the Orbot. Her impressive torso anatomy hung dangerously close to my head. Had I been operational at that moment, the view would've been quite... Can I say 'titillating'? I guess not. Ahem. Sadly, I wasn't operational.

Marta pulled out a small square device from her belt pack and plugged a thin wire into my chest. After a few seconds, she was presented with a reading.

'There's no operating system, no neural network activity and nothing in his memory.'

'Oh my Bod,' said Ray, 'is he... you know... dead?'

'Don't be a nerdumsklepp, son,' said Col. 'He's an Orbot. He was never alive in the first place. Well, not in the traditional sense.'

He had a point. I would've said that too, had I been there. But then, if I had been there, I wouldn't have been dead, would I? And I'm not, so...

Hahahaha! This is getting confusing even for me. And I've died before, if you remember? Better to just stick to the facts. Jolly good.

'So where's his personality gone then?' said Jeff. 'You know, his... soul, for want of a better word?'

'Has he been wiped? Or corrupted?' added Ray.

Marta looked at her device and ran a few scans. She looked up, shaking her head.

'No, it all seems to be in working order, but there aren't any files or data there. It's as if someone's downloaded his program to another machine.'

'But where is it now? And more to the point, how did this happen to him?' said Jeff, still none the wiser.

'I don't know. Where did you find him?'

'Outside,' said Col, pointing in a vaguely outsidey direction. 'He was in a CommShop. His finger was still connected to a terminal.'

'I see,' said Marta. She unplugged the device and

replaced it in her belt. 'Looks like he escaped by uploading himself elsewhere.'

Jeff gaped in disappointed awe.

'What a flipping chicken! He did a flit on us! Typical!'

Ray shrugged in both defeat and acceptance of the facts.

'Oh well. No use flying over spilt milk. What are we going to do with him now?'

Col picked up the empty shell and dragged it over to the seating area at the rear of the ship. He sat it down and positioned the arms and legs carefully at the table, like a child playing with a doll.

'He can stay here, I suppose. If we ever find out where his program went, we might need to put him back in his body.'

Urgh! I just had another shudder. My first out-of-body experience!

Jeff was getting impatient to trace his loved ones. He walked over to the cockpit area and stood by the arch.

'Right, so what now? Grid's gone, the ship's knackered, and we've still got no idea where my wife and my baby are!'

'Col and Ray came over. Ray put a hand on Jeff's shoulder.

'I know. But we're getting there. Look, we've got help now – a galactic agent! She'll be able to help us, surely?'

Marta and Herman stood by the main door of the spacecraft. Herman pushed the button to open it.

'Actually,' said Marta, ushering Herman through the door, 'my work here is done. I've saved the galaxy more times than you've had – well, whatever it is you humans have regularly – and now I've found my Herman, I'm finished with it all.'

'What?' said Jeff, who'd heard perfectly well. 'You can't just take him and leave us! The whole planet's been invaded, and...'

'The whole galactic sector has been invaded,' interrupted Marta.

'Yeah? Well I didn't know that. But I'm talking about the love of my life! And our baby – out there somewhere, alone and defenceless!'

Defenceless. Hah! If only he knew.

Marta stopped and considered his words. He did say, 'the love of my life', didn't he? She knew what it felt like to be separated from your soulmate. She gritted her teeth in defiance of her compassion.

'I'm sorry. No. I really can't help you. We have to go.'

She turned and left the ship. Herman was standing in the plaza waiting for her amid the scattered bodies of the slain Macadamian soldiers. Jeff, Col and Ray watched as they walked to Marta's hover car and drove away, heading for their new future out there, somewhere.

Ray sighed.

'That's a shame. I rather liked Herman. Sounds like he's a bit under the green thumb though.'

'I quite liked her, too,' said Jeff.

Col placed his hands on the shoulders of Jeff and Ray.

'Let him go. You have to realise that they've both been through a lot. He's been a slave for years, and she's apparently fought her way across half the galaxy to find him. The very fact that they managed to get back together is nothing short of miraculaculus. They deserve their happy ending, even if it deprives us of ours.'

Jeff huffed again.

'I think I'm going to be sick.'

Ray sat down at the controls and began to push buttons, humming to himself.

'What are you up to?' asked Jeff. 'The ship's knackered, remember?'

'I know,' said Ray. 'But I repaired the *Penguin* before; maybe if I can find out what's wrong with this one, I can fix it too?'

'Sorry to burst your parade, son,' said Col, 'but didn't it take you the best part of a decade to repair the Marshmallow Penguin?'

'Yes it did, actually.'

'So what hope have you got now?'

'A little more than you pair of naysayers, it seems.'

Ray had a point. Jeff and Col looked suitably ashamed in the light of Ray's positive attitude.

'All righty, Ray. What's the plan then? Can she be fixed up?'

'According to these damage reports, the drive unit took a hit from outside. The shot punctured a tiny hole in the outer hull...' began Ray.

'A tiny hole? Can we plug it up?' offered Jeff.

'...a tiny hole that ruptured a plasma conduit...'

'We could patch the conduit then,' said Jeff.

'The conduit leaked liquid drive plasma onto the warp manifold shielding...'

'We can clean that off, surely?'

'... which dissolved and melted into the entire drive system, turning it into a solid lump of useless junk.'

'We could... Oh bugger.'

'Indeed,' said Ray, flopping back into the chair. 'We're stuffed. Perhaps we should start walking?'

Col called from the rear of the ship, where he was crawling around on the floor as if he'd lost an eye.

'Don't bother.'

Ray swivelled his seat around to face his dad.

'Have you got any better ideas?'

'I do, as a matter of fact.'

Jeff and Ray clambered out of the pilot seats and headed over to Col, who had removed a large square panel from the cabin floor. He pointed down into the cavity.

'Storage space. These deluxe models are a little roomier than the standard flyers. Your singing friend Mister Astley has expensive tastes. Look!'

Jeff and Ray peered down and saw a pair of smaller vehicles that looked a little like jetskis.

'What are they?' asked Jeff.

'Flykes,' said Ray. 'Flying bikes. They're used for racing and messing about in the sea.'

'Are they tricky to ride?' asked Jeff.

Col shook his head.

'It's like riding a bike, actually. Literally.'

'We can use these to get back into the city!' said Ray. 'I'm sure we can find Tailback and the baby in no time at all!

'Sounds good to me, matey!' said Jeff, brightening up.

'Ah. Just one problem, chaps...' said Col, crossing his arms.

'Let me guess,' sighed Jeff, 'No fuel?'

'No. They've got fuel all right. But there are three of us and only two flykes. They only seat one person, don't they?'

'That's not a problem,' said Jeff.

Ten minutes later, Col was sitting in the pilot's seat, tapping his fingers as he watched Jeff and Ray speeding away into the distance. He looked over at the shell that used to contain me, and although technically I wasn't present, he could almost see the slightly mocking grin on its plastic face.

'And you can shut up, too,' he said.

Charming.

chapter nine

Shump Around

'Behind every great man is a woman rolling her eyes.
Jim Carrey

Jeff and Ray rode their flykes through the streets at trouser-dampening speeds. It took surprisingly little time to master the controls, and Jeff couldn't help likening the craft to a small motor scooter that he had once had, only with a bit more poke. He couldn't read the alien hieroglyphics that flashed up on the steering column, but he guessed that this was a speedometer. Then again, he didn't really want to know that he was hitting nearly a hundred miles an hour without helmet, seat belt or insurance. He just hung on and tried not to swallow any flies. Well, not any big ones, anyway. He was getting a taste for the little ones.

The closer they got to the city centre, the more both men got the distinct feeling that things were not as they seemed. Having seen the arrival of a lot of Macadamian ships, they had expected an increased military presence. Yet there was none. The streets were just as quiet as before, but there were no loudspeaker announcements about curfews, no foot patrols, and all the major roads were unguarded. Not a checkpoint in sight.

Ray slowed down and Jeff managed to catch him up.

'Jeff! It's too quiet!' called Ray, disturbing the quiet.

'I know,' said Jeff. 'I was just wondering where all the nuts were.'

'Do you suppose that green agent, Marta, wiped them out?'

'I dunno, matey. She's good but she's not exactly an army.'

'I wouldn't like to tangle with her.'

Jeff sniggered.

'I'd like to. She is pretty fit…'

Ray rolled his eyes.

'I'll keep the paramedics on speed dial, just in case.'

Ray accelerated and Jeff followed. They soon got to the hypertrain station, where they had been loaded onto Cleggeron's moving freakshow.

Ray parked his flyke and walked up to the archway that led to the platform. It was unmanned and the gates were open. Jeff followed, looking around cautiously. Despite the apparent emptiness of the place, he still felt the need to tread quietly.

Ray had turned a corner and disappeared. Jeff huffed and quickened his tiptoeing.

'Oi, Ray!' he hissed. 'Not so fast! We don't know who or what…'

He froze as he turned the corner.

'Oh bugger.'

Standing in front of him, was Ray held by the huge, throat-crushing hands of Gwaggle and Twong. Alongside them was their boss, one very sour, serious, two-faced Nivid Cleggeron.

'Lovely day for a ride, eh, Jeff?'

'Niv! Fancy meeting you here!' said Jeff, foolishly trying to keep the conversation light. All Ray could offer was a feeble choking noise.

'You lied to me, Jeffrey,' said Cleggeron, stepping forward. 'You lied, betrayed and left me. I thought we worked well together, but that's what I get for trusting an Earthlet.'

'Sorry, Niv,' said Jeff, 'but I wasn't your partner, I was your prisoner. We all were. What did you expect me to do?'

'I expected you to be honest and genuine. But no, you humans always lie and deceive, don't you? We Toreenians have one face for expressions, the other for intentions!'

'And they're both ugly as sin, so suck on that. Plus you're a lying, slave-trading obnoxious little git. So why don't you put Ray down and deal with me. Or are you too much of a chicken, four eyes?'

I guess you could safely say that Jeff was feeling the strain.

Cleggeron had never been insulted like that in his life. He'd always lived a life of easy superiority; he wasn't used to someone standing up to him. Plus, he had no idea what a 'chicken' was, though it didn't sound pleasant. This was new, it was uncomfortable and it simply wouldn't do.

He motioned to his mindless minders. Gwaggle tensed his arm and threw Ray at Jeff, knocking them both over like skittles.

'Shut it, Spooner,' said Cleggeron, folding his arms decisively. 'You've had all the chances you're going to

171

get from me. I should have kept you caged up with the rest of the freaks. Rip them both to shreds!'

Ray wasn't moving. Jeff wasn't even sure that he was breathing. And as the seconds slowed and the hulking brutes stomped forward, murderous intent in their beady eyes, it dawned on him that maybe his big mouth had finally said too much – that he'd killed his best friend, seconds before he was about to die himself.

The bodyguards grabbed his arms so tightly that he could feel the veins collapsing under the pressure. His hands tingled with the rush of blood straining to burst out of the fingertips, and the pain hit him like a sharp spike being driven into his brain. 'I'm sorry, Ray,' was his last thought before all thoughts were squeezed out of him.

Gwaggle and Twong grinned as they pulled in opposite directions. Cleggeron watched intently, listening for the satisfying snapping of bone.

There was a loud series of cracks.

Gwaggle and Twong froze, each bearing four large smoking holes in their heads and bodies. They fell to the ground, releasing their grip on Jeff, who himself fell flat on his back in agony.

Both of Cleggeron's jaws dropped simultaneously. He cowered at the sight of Marta Vina standing there, holding no less than six laser pistols in her hands and her back-tentacles. She had a hundred witty lines ready for a moment like this, but she decided to save them all for someone more deserving.

Cleggeron's faces suddenly adopted warm smiles, ones that signalled his intention to smarm his way out of this situation. Unfortunately for him, Marta was not some unsuspecting fool. She knew everything about him and what he'd done to Herman.

'Listen, can't we just talk about—' he began.

She opened fire again, blasting the surprised Toreenian with all of her six guns. He practically exploded in a shower of dark brown, slimy blood. It looked like someone had thrown a bottle of chocolate sauce against a wall. Only not quite as tasty.

'No, we can't,' said Marta.

A hover car arrived. Herman jumped out and ran over to Jeff and Ray, who were both groaning quietly on the floor, not yet fully aware of what had just happened.

'Mein freunds! Are you all right?'

Jeff was the first to win the consciousness race.

'My whole life flashed before my eyes. It was pretty crap, actually. Is that you, Herman?'

'Ja. It ist me. We came looking for you.'

'Ray! Is Ray OK?'

'He's going to be fine,' said Marta, who was already tending to the bearded barber. She waved a small vial of something under his nose, which brought him back to full consciousness in a matter of seconds. He sat up quickly, then realised it was a mistake to move so fast.

'Argh! Ouch! Ow! My head! My neck! My everything!'

'Blimey,' said Jeff. 'You had me worried for a minute!'

'You were worried? I had myself worried! I thought this was the afterlife for a second, and I was really disappointed!' said Ray.

'Why are we surrounded by dead people?' said Jeff, finally noticing the carnage.

'They've been eliminated. It's what I do,' said Marta, standing up and putting her guns and tentacles away.

'Yeah, I can see that!' said Jeff, helping Ray to his feet. 'How did you get here?'

'In the hover car,' said Herman.

'Not you, her!' said Ray, looking at Marta.

Marta stepped up, grabbing the attention of Jeff and Ray.

'I have another skill. It's not something I do often, nor do I like to advertise it. Gives me a tactical advantage.'

'What's that then? Are you some kind of a ninja or something?' asked Jeff.

'What's a ninja?' asked Marta.

'Stealthy assassin. They sneak about unseen and unheard. Pretty cool actually.'

Marta shook her head.

'Not quite.'

Shump.

She disappeared. Instantly. Into thin air. Not a trace. Jeff and Ray blinked in disbelief. Needless to say, Herman wasn't amazed – he'd seen the trick before.

'Behind you.'

They turned around to see her standing there calmly with a smile on her face. Jeff's jaw dropped again.

'You can turn invisible? That's incredible!'

'No, it's not invisibility. It's called "Shumping".'

'Shumping? What the hell's that when it's at home?'

'Short-Burst Quantum Jumping. I can teleport myself at will.'

'Really?' said Ray. 'Doesn't it involve any machinery or equipment then?'

'Only a couple of tiny cerebral implants. Most of it's done by willpower.'

'Implants.' Jeff nudged Ray in the ribs with his elbow.

'Not those kind,' said Marta.

'Ignore him,' said Ray. 'So do all you galactic agents know how to do this then? It's awfully useful.'

Marta shook her head.

'Only the lucky ones. Some of us have the ability to focus so acutely on our molecular structure that we can harness the nuclear forces that make up every living thing. Our implants help us to direct the molecules to any nearby location that we can envisage. We shump out of existence and reform once we've moved. It's not something I can do repeatedly though. Takes a lot of concentration.'

Herman smiled and reached out for her green hand.

'Ah, *mein liebling*, she hast so many *wunderbar* skills,' he gushed.

'That's totally mental, that is,' said Jeff, still amazed.

'Almost. Apart from the implants,' said Marta, missing his point entirely.

Ray looked at the mess of bodies around him and tried not to throw up.

'Was all this really necessary?'

'You were about to be killed,' said Marta, back to business. 'I stopped them. Get over it.'

'And we're grateful, of course, but couldn't you have, I dunno, stunned them or something?'

'I don't do "stun". There's no point.'

Ray knew he wasn't going to get anywhere with this. What had been done was done. Pretty permanently, in fact.

'We've got to go. Any idea where Tailback and the baby could be?'

'Ja. Well, kind of,' said Herman.

'Kind of?'

'While we were travelling, we picked up on the military radio transmissions. Something artificial ist approaching the Royal Palace.'

'Artificial?' asked Jeff. 'You mean an Orbot? My Tailback?'

'Well, sort of...' said Herman, trying and failing to play the awkwardness down.

'Sort of?'

'It fits the description of an Orbot. But there's no reason to believe it's your partner,' said Marta. 'From what we picked up, this Orbot is a thousand feet tall and wiping out everything in its path.'

'Blimey Charlie!' said Jeff. 'I know she's got a temper on her, but a thousand feet tall? How the bleeding hell did that happen?'

'I have no idea. It was tracked heading towards the palace ever since it came out of the sea.'

'The sea?' asked Ray.

'Oh my good gawd!' said Jeff. 'That's where we last saw her!'

'That might explain why we haven't seen any soldiers out here. What about the baby?' asked Ray. 'Anything about him?'

'I think that *ist* the baby,' said Herman.

'Right, we've got to get to the palace. That's the only thing for it,' said Jeff heading for his flyke.

'Erm, wait a minute!' called Ray. 'Did you not hear the bit about this thing wiping out everything in its path?'

'Heard it, matey. But the way I see it, that thing might be my son. I've got to find out!'

He jumped on his flyke and raced away, heading in the direction of the palace.

Ray turned to Marta and Herman.

'Well, you came back for a reason. Are you still willing to help us? I won't mind if you don't want to. You've done enough.'

Herman and Marta looked at each other briefly. They were of the same mind.

'Looks like I've got one last mission to complete before any of us can get some peace!' said Marta.

'These humans, eh?' said Ray. 'Can't live with 'em, can't... live with 'em.'

They headed for the hover car and followed Jeff as fast as they could.

chapter ten
Tempestuous Temper Tantrums

'War does not determine who is right – only who is left.'
Bertrand Russell

In the Macadamian-occupied palace on Kangazang, a siren sounded. A lone soldier named Private Nutt jumped off his seat when he saw what was on his surveillance monitor. He then jumped off his mini step ladder, which was there to help him get into his seat in the first place, and when he finally got to ground level, he ran along the hallway as fast as his stumpy legs could carry him.

There was no time for procedure and protocol. He barged the throne room doors open and frightened the life out of Colonel Kernel, who was just having an afternoon nut-nap.

'Colonel Kernel! Colonel Kernel!' gasped Nutt. Which was a hilarious thing to hear someone gasp, in actual fact.

'Eh? What is it, man?' said Kernel, trying to wake himself up rapidly. 'What's the meaning of this intrusion?'

'We're under attack, sir! It's big, probably over a hundred shells tall!'

'Under attack?' sputtered Kernel. 'What's attacking?

I hear no gunfire!'

'That's because it's eaten all the guns!'

'You jest, boy. Send the fleet out, then.'

'I sent the fleet out, sir! It's been eaten too! That's why there aren't any guns going off!' Kernel looked utterly bewildered. He wasn't sure if this was serious or some kind of practical joke. He required solid facts.

'Right, Nutt, calm down and tell me what you saw.'

'It's a baby, sir – a giant silver baby! Stomping around, eating things! People, mostly!'

Kernel remained bewildered. He was time-served, battle hardened and dry roasted; he was well aware that most of his adversaries would be bigger than he was, but surely not... younger at the same time?

He jumped off his cushion pile and went over to the huge throne room windows, followed by Private Nutt, who was in danger of cracking under the strain.

Looking out over the landscape, Colonel Kernel could only just make out a vague silvery figure on the horizon. He thrust a hand out to his side.

'Telescope! Now!' he barked.

seen for miles, inspiring the tourists.

Colonel Kernel breathed a sign of relief.

'You nutjob, Nutt! That's no giant baby, it's just... Oh my sainted shell!'

His vision had been obscured by ErHuer, who dwarfed the statue of Rick, and was approaching fast.

Kernel watched in horror as ErHuer swung his arms around, catching the remaining Macadamian fighter craft, which were instantly absorbed into the sparkling colossus. The ground shook as he stamped his feet on the armed forces below. The statue of Rick wobbled.

179

ErHuer stomped ever closer. Rick began to lean over to one side, the metal squealing loudly (but rather fittingly, in perfect pitch).

ErHuer's foot came down beside the steep hill upon which Rick was currently standing, and the hill began to shrink as it was absorbed.

Rick finally fell over.

Rick rolled.

Priceless!

Deep within ErHuer, safe from the carnage outside, Tailback held on as her son bucked around. She tuned into his moods and detected immensely strong feelings of determination, driven by anger and a deep confusion stemming from not knowing his real purpose.

'Ah, here we are!' said ErHuer.

Tailback noticed that his somewhat formal, logical dialogue had evolved somewhat.

'This is where those horrid little nutjobs are based, Mother. Let's pop in for a cup of tea and a sit down, shall we?'

'What are you going to do?' asked Tailback.

Before her was a scene of utter non-devastation. There was no rubble or ruined buildings; the city had been scraped clean, right down to the ground. It looked quite neat actually. The city had been flattened, smashed and wiped up again. ErHuer hadn't left a crumb.

In front of her she could see the Kangazanian Palace. It was the only remaining building for miles around. Surrounding it were a thousand Macadamian ground troops, firing uselessly at the invader. ErHuer simply fed on the projectiles and laser beams, lapping up the energy and raw materials they provided.

Through the chest window, Tailback spotted Colonel Kernel staring up at her.

'Son! Stop! You mustn't destroy any more! Please!' she begged.

ErHuer paused.

'I beg your pardon? Listen, Mum, these invaders have no right to be here. They've taken over the whole planet, not to mention another nineteen others in this sector, enslaved all the people and taken Dad, Uncle Col and Uncle Ray. And this horrid little chap is behind it all. Let's have a word, shall we?'

Before Tailback could protest, her son's huge hand had reached out and torn off the roof of the palace. As the roof crumbled into thousands of tiles, each one was sucked into the hand and fingers of her son like crumbs into a vacuum cleaner. He scooped up Colonel Kernel and Private Nutt into his palm and lifted them out of the ruined building and closer to his face.

Colonel Kernel stood his ground. Or at least his palm, for that was where he stood, while Private Nutt had curled up into a ball and was gibbering uncontrollably. At least Nutt had the right idea.

'Right, you diminutive despot,' said ErHuer at a deafening volume. 'It's time you packed up your entire army and sodded off back to whichever nuthouse you came from.'

He did sound a little like Jeff Spooner, in actual fact. Microchip off the old blockhead.

Kernel looked up at ErHuer's huge mirror-ball face and pointed his swagger stick directly at him in an attempt to intimidate the as-yet un-intimidated behemoth.

'Absolutely not. I represent the entire Macadamian

forces, under direct instructions from the High Dictators, and I take my orders from them and them alone. So you – whatever your name is – listen up and listen well: Cease your attack immediately or face the consequences!'

ErHuer raised the cranial ridges where his eyebrows, if he'd had some, would have been. Then he threw his head back and laughed so loudly that the sound waves knocked birds out of the sky.

'Attack?' asked ErHuer incredulously. 'I haven't attacked anyone or anything! This is just growing up, feeding. A light snack! I haven't even got to the main course yet!'

Tailback felt rising waves of arrogance and anger. She waved her arms to get the colonel's attention.

'Colonel! Listen to him – he's telling the truth! Give up now before it's too late. I don't know what he's capable of!'

Colonel Kernel was quite surprised to see an Orbot imprisoned within the huge creature. Unfortunately, his ego was far more developed than his brain.

'Aha! So you're the one driving this robot! You're the pilot!'

He pointed his stick at Tailback, redirecting his attempt at intimidation. So far, it had been about as successful as a Hoppa in a three-legged race.

'I'm not a pilot! And this is not a robot! This is my son!' cried Tailback, desperately trying to cut through the wall of confusion.

'Your son? Nonsense! Desist immediately! We still occupy twenty planets in this sector alone! One word from me and we can eliminate entire populations. Don't push me, robot!'

'ErHuer!' said ErHuer.

'Bless you,' said Kernel, instinctively.

ErHuer brought him a little closer.

'No. My name is ErHuer, little being, and my mum there is telling the truth. Don't try strong-arm tactics with me, Colonel. I promise you, you won't win this argument, battle or, indeed, war.'

At that moment, Private Nutt got to his feet and looked at his Colonel.

'You can stick your army! I quit!' he yelled, diving off ErHuer's hand.

Tailback saw his parachute open as he fell, and felt relief for the little soldier who, like most of the Macadamian troops, were brainwashed into following orders from this walnut-headed wacko. It looked like he'd broken free of it. Good for him.

Tailback realised that trying to act as a mediator in this clash of the titans was quite pointless. The two opponents seemed to possess equally gigantic egos despite their differing size. Despite the colonel's maniacal devotion to military conquest, she didn't want his followers to suffer any more casualties. But she also didn't want her son to be harmed by a deranged dictator with twenty occupied worlds in his grip. More than anything else, she wished Jeff was there with her. She still didn't know where he was or even if he was alive at all.

ErHuer must have sensed his mother's emotional state, because he felt a sudden flush of sympathy. He could hardly believe the words he found himself saying when he opened his mouth:

'Come on, Colonel. This is pointless. Why don't we forget the whole thing and talk it through over a nice cup of tea like

183

grown-ups, eh? You don't want to be destroyed, and I don't really want to do any more destroying. We can all get along. After all, the cosmos is big enough for the both of us.'

That felt strange to ErHuer. But it was testament to his mother, who had learned so much about love and life from Jeff Spooner. See? He wasn't totally useless.

Even the colonel was taken aback by this sudden change of tack.

ErHuer gently sat down on the ground and crossed his legs. He lowered his hand and placed the colonel down on the ground, unharmed.

Tailback flopped to her knee joints in relief. She could detect that her son was genuine in his compassion. She watched the colonel standing there, and was surprised to see him remain in front of them, as opposed to running away as fast as he could.

ErHuer leaned forward so that he could see the colonel's tiny face more clearly.

'Colonel, if you had in your possession a bomb so effective, so powerful that to detonate it would destroy every living organism in the Universe except yours, would you allow its use?'

Kernel rubbed his underbite in deep thought.

'Hmm. Interesting... ' he pondered. 'Yes, I *would* do it! Such power would set me up above the gods! And through my armies, I shall have that power!'

'Colonel! Please don't do this!' cried Tailback, banging her fists against the glass.

But Colonel Kernel remained stupidly steadfast and arrogantly adamant. He pulled a radio from his belt and looked up at ErHuer, then Tailback, who stood with her hands pressed up against the glass, shaking her head in desperation.

'You lose, robots. Prepare to face annihilation.'

He pressed the communicator switch on the radio.

'All legion commanders! This is the colonel. Execute 'Order Sixty-Seven' on my command.'

ErHuer tilted his head sideways, wondering what this order entailed. Suddenly, he could detect the accumulated waves of fear coming through the radio waves and InfoHex transmissions. Never had there been such an outpouring of terror and dismay all at once. ErHuer absorbed it all. He realised in that moment what was about to happen.

And he felt... sick.

Twenty populated worlds in that sector of the galaxy were about to be depopulated at an alarming rate. The occupying forces of the Macadamians would slaughter billions of men, women and children simultaneously. No debate, no second thoughts, no mercy. The colonel took a deep breath as he gave the command.

'All Legions, Open f... '

'NO.'

It was ErHuer that spoke.

Not in protest or fear, but a simple, clear command that illustrated his omnipotent will.

Faced with the concept of genocide in astronomical proportions, instigated by a person who showed no regard for anything else in the Universe other than himself, ErHuer suddenly realised that life, not death, was the way forward. And those who failed to grasp this had to be stopped.

Within milliseconds, ErHuer disassembled himself, flooding into the planet's surface, utilising the trillions of tons of matter and energy at his disposal. But he hadn't considered Tailback: She fell out of the chest cavity as it disintegrated and plummeted down to the ground, where she smashed into pieces, scattering limbs and broken parts everywhere. Her head remained connected to her torso. Still conscious, she looked up into the sky.

Colonel Kernel gasped, unable to complete his order. He watched the unique hybrid life form come of age. Thousands of thin silver strands shot into the sky, like spider's silk, crossing the stars at light speed. Everything they came into contact with, from microscopic dust particles to comets, was absorbed by the strands, speeding their journeys. Then, when one of the twenty occupied planets came into range, the strands fanned out, encapsulating the entire world of in a white web. Kangazang was also plunged it into sudden total darkness. From a distance the entire galactic sector looked like it had been shrouded in spider's silk. Kangazang was plunged it into sudden total darkness, followed by every other occupied planet.

One such planet was the pretty blue world of Laurandishax. The terrified population all feared the worst when the Macadamian soldiers drew their guns and prepared to open fire. But the order never came. Instead, their skies flashed silver for a moment before night suddenly swallowed their world up. The population of the planet cried out in confusion and fear before the sky fractured into trillions of silver crystals that rained down over the whole surface. But this was not rain, nor was it any other explicable weather condition. It was living projectiles, bullets with their own minds, seeking out oppression and hostility, driven by an angry young man who would not allow the slaughter of innocents.

The living bullets flew right through the bodies of the occupying soldiers, shattering them like skittles made of glass. The bewildered Shaxian people were unarmed, standing in shock as they watched every single hostile soldier, gun, tank, plane and bomb get ripped to shreds by the unforgiving silver rain.

The process took just under two minutes, after which time, the bullets bounced back up to the heavens and congregated there as a bright white sky, vigilant and sentient, illuminating and watching over the stunned people of the planet, now saved from certain death.

And the same thing happened on nineteen other worlds: the Macamian military fell to the unrelenting showers of destruction save for just two of its soldiers: Colonel Kernel and Private Nutt, who stood there in the grounds of the Kangazanian Palace, watching ErHuer display his undeniable superiority with a temper tantrum on a phenomenal scale.

In two minutes, the entire race, the total population of Macadamia was utterly erased from the Universe.

As the sky shimmered and buzzed under the watchful presence of ErHuer's new form, Tailback heard a sound and turned her head to see Jeff arrive on his flyke. He drove it right into the palace grounds and leapt off it, landing by her side.

'Hello, Jeff. I've missed you,' said Tailback weakly. Her eyelids were twitching uncontrollably, and some of her facial modules weren't working correctly.

Jeff picked her up and cradled her in his arms.

'Tail! What happened to you? What's going on?'

'Our... baby, Jeff. He's all grown up. Look.'

'Grown up? He's only three days old! Where is he?'

She turned her head to indicate the bright sky.

'What the hell is that? I thought he was some giant bleedin' monster!' spluttered Jeff, in what was probably the highest level of confusion he'd ever known.

'He was. But he's saved us all. The Macadamians were about to wipe out every planet in this sector. He stopped them!'

In the distance, Ray, Herman and Marta arrived in the hover car. It's a minor detail, but it was hilarious to see Ray and Herman clambering out of the hovering, bouncy vehicle like newborn cattle, while Marta leapt up and out gracefully, like a heavily-armed ballet dancer. You should've been there. She somersaulted perfectly, landing on her feet and running over to Jeff and Tailback, extracting her tentacles from her back, each one wrapped around a blaster pistol. She pointed all six guns at Colonel Kernel and Private Nutt.

'You're not going anywhere, Colonel,' she said firmly. And she was right.

Kernel jumped in shock.

'Argh! An octopus with guns! Do something, Nutt!' he yelped.

'Forget it, mate!' said Nutt, throwing down his rifle and ripping the rank stripes off his shoulder armour. 'This day has been weird enough!'

Considering that he and his Colonel were the last two remaining Macadamians army left in the Universe , the young soldier's choice of self-preservation was a sensible one. He scampered off into the distance, gibbering uncontrollably, until his existence was noticed – and subsequently terminated – by ErHuer's planet-wide consciousness. A blast of the angry white lightning fell

188

from the sky, the deadly bullets chopping the hapless Macadamian into nut-gravel. Without a large portion of ice cream nearby, it was, in my opinion, a terrible waste.

Marta ignored it. It was Kernel that she wanted to keep in her sights.

'All alone now, matey,' said Jeff, trying to retain his composure despite the incredibly disturbing weirdness he had just witnessed. 'Your little game of soldiers is all over. You've got a lot to answer for, nutjob.'

Like most tin-pot dictators, Colonel Kernel didn't know when to quit. He stood his ground defiantly, looking up at Jeff and the green, literally heavily-armed beauty before him.

'If you're expecting me to surrender, forget it! I control this planet now! The prophecy has been fulfilled at last. And I, Colonel Kernel, supreme commander of the glorious Macadamian Empire, will—'

'Pack it in, nutjob!'

Jeff sent him across the plaza with a kick that would've made David Beckham proud. Kernel even curved in mid-air too. He hit the ground hard, sustaining a number of serious fractures, and fell unconscious. He wasn't going to be a threat to anyone again.

'Impressive,' said Marta.

Jeff went back to his beloved Tailback, who was fading fast. He picked her up gently, holding her torso, head and one arm, like they were in a disturbing ventriloquist act.

'Jeff… scared. Power… two percent,' she whispered.

Jeff choked back the tears.

'Don't try to talk. We'll get you fixed up, don't worry. I'll…'

'No,' said Tailback. 'Damage… extensive. Return to manufacturer. Shutdown imminent. Look after… son.'

'Don't go!' wailed Jeff, looking around for assistance. Ray came over and spoke gently.

'It's no use, Jeff. She's going. The damage she's sustained can't be fixed.'

'What if we got her to Orbitron to look at her? Could they help?'

'She'd be gone by the time we got there. I'm sorry Jeff.'

Jeff looked down at his robotic girlfriend.

'Love… you… Je…'

Her eyelids slowly slid shut, and the last of her powered movements ebbed away. For an artificial life form, she'd grown considerably, learned about life, love – even given birth. But all things inevitably return to a state of stillness. She was running on minimal battery power now, which wasn't enough to sustain any movement, and even that was due to expire in a matter of minutes, leaving her truly dead.

Jeff sniffed as his tears fell onto her still face, and Ray also wiped a tear from his eye.

Up above, the planet-encompassing cloud that was ErHuer felt the loss of his mother. He rippled and shrank, pouring himself down onto the surface of Kangazang like a waterfall that took the form of the silver giant that he had previously been.

His voice was calm, but with a tone of sadness.

'Can you hear me, Mother?'

Jeff looked up at ErHuer through watery eyes.

'She's gone, son.'

'Gone? No! I refuse to accept it. She must not be gone.

I need her to stay here, to teach me about—'

'Don't you get it?' yelled Jeff, his temper rising, 'She's dead! There's nothing anyone can do!'

'No. I deny it. I can—'

'You can just stop it. Give it up, will you? You've done enough, son! It's all over.'

'He's right,' said Ray. 'Listen to your father.'

ErHuer was momentarily stunned. Here was his father – the Jeff Spooner that he'd heard about but not yet met, and here was he being told off like a little child.

'No, Daddy dearest. I will not give it up. Where were you when Mum and I needed you? Judging by my records, you were probably imbibing alcohol. Or consuming hybrid meat and vegetable-based snack foods. Not with your partner and child, at any rate!'

Jeff looked incredulously at the silver shape and handed Tailback's still form over to Ray.

'Now hang a banger, mate. There was nowhere I would have rather been than with you and your mother. But I was captured by those nutjobs, and I had to save mine, and everyone else's skins. Who do you think you're talking to?'

'I'm talking to a loser named Jeff Spooner, it seems.'

'Right! That's it. You've gone too far. You're not too big to go over my knee, sunshine!'

Ray leaned in.

'He is, actually.'

ErHuer crouched down on one knee, so that his head was a lot closer to the tiny people on the ground.

'Just you try it, Dad. And see what happens!'

Jeff knew that, despite his son's immense size and godlike abilities, he had to be disciplined. But how does one discipline a being of such power?

191

He thought for a moment and mumbled something.

'What was that?' asked ErHuer.

Jeff mumbled again.

ErHuer crouched even tighter, bringing his giant face level with Jeff.

'Say it to my face!' he boomed, ruffling Jeff's hair with his gale force breath.

Jeff slapped him. Right across the nose. The effect was akin to a gnat landing on an elephant.

ErHuer flinched.

Not that it hurt him in any way, but the shock of being struck in anger by his father was something he had never thought would happen. The sheer audacity of it was difficult to compute.

He looked at Jeff in wordless amazement for a moment, and considered whether to swat his father like the aforementioned gnat, instantly removing the annoying little being from existence, or to burst out crying. He'd never been struck like that before. He'd been shot, had missiles flung at him, but his dad had lashed out in anger. This was new. And suddenly it did hurt. He raised himself up to his full height and opened his arms out. He wailed so loudly that everyone could feel their skulls vibrating. It was a wail of anguish, sadness and most of all, frustrated anger.

'That's it! I'm done with this planet. All I wanted was to grow up unhindered, but nobody would let me. I've been since birth, lost my mother, and now I've been physically assaulted by my so-called father. Let me show you what that feels like!'

The planet started shaking as ErHuer began to sink into the ground. Cracks appeared in the concrete, running across the plaza like lightning bolts.

Ray and Jeff staggered back, struggling to keep their footing.

'He's going to split the planet in half! We're doomed!' yelled Ray.

'Oi!' called Jeff to his son. 'Pack it in!'

But ErHuer wasn't listening any more. He sank further still, now up to his neck in the ground. Jeff could make out an anguished expression as he drove himself like a wedge into the crust of the planet.

Herman clung onto Marta, desperately sharing their last moments together. But then Marta pushed him away and ran over to the hover car. Herman sat on the ground, utterly confused as he watched his beloved secret agent in action. There was nothing she could do, surely?

Marta grabbed the case of F-Bombs from the car and ran back to the spot where ErHuer was descending into the ground. She hopped and jumped over the widening cracks until she got to his face.

'Vot ist she doing?' called Herman to Ray, 'The bombs will kill us all!'

Ray screamed back.

'Does it really matter now? The planet's had it anyway!'

'Look!' called Jeff. He pointed to Marta.

The green agent reached ErHuer's head and leapt up, landing directly on top. She cast a glimpse at Herman and played her hunch.

Shump.

She disappeared. Everyone looked around, but she was nowhere to be seen. Even ErHuer had no idea where she was.

And then he found her.

She materialised inside his chest cavity, where he'd previously kept Tailback prisoner. Quickly, she opened the case and used her tentacles to prime the deadly cubes to a critical point. They hummed like a nest of irate bees as she dropped them onto the ground. Then she took the last one and gave it a final twist.

She dropped the F-Bomb.

With nanoseconds to spare, Marta shumped back out of ErHuer and onto the surface of Kangazang, diving onto the floor in anticipation of a very big bang.

The resulting noise was so loud it made thunder sound like a mouse fart. The entire continent shook violently, and Jeff, Ray and Herman bounced around like popcorn on a hot plate.

ErHuer was now so powerful that his molecular bindings were strong enough to hold the blast in, but when the four cubes detonated, they totally scrambled him internally.

The organic parts of him were superheated, breaking down into little more than dust. ErHuer screamed in pain and anger as he registered what was happening. He pulled all his remaining non-organic molecules together and re-formed into a smaller figure, only ten or fifteen feet tall, that staggered forward as though drunk, and then toppled over, crashing down onto the surface, stunned temporarily.

Jeff and Ray saw most of it through the dust cloud. Getting to their feet, they whooped and cheered at what looked like a victory.

Then they heard a scream.

'HERMAN!'

It was Marta. She sat there on her knees, gaping in terror at the sight before her.

ErHuer had landed on Herman. Jeff raced over and dragged ErHuer's groaning, still stunned figure away from the fallen aquaphibioid. There was no movement or sign of life. And the sight wasn't pleasant. He laid still, his lower half turned to a grisly fish paste.

Marta roared in anger. She dived onto ErHuer and unleashed a salvo of jabs and punches into his head. ErHuer was now regaining consciousness, but the vicious beating had no effect on him. He stood up and threw her aside like a snot-filled handkerchief. She tumbled across the dusty plaza and sat blinking through teary eyes as the silver figure addressed the gathering before him.

'So this is what it's come down to then, has it? Death and destruction. What about me? I'm not even a week old and I've already seen more of it than I care to mention!'

Jeff called up at his son.

'You caused most of it yourself, son! You can't blame people for trying to defend themselves!'

'I was surviving, *Father*. You know, doing my best to stay alive and get though life despite insurmountable odds. You weren't there, were you? No! Out of the picture! Part-time parent, that's you! Well, I've done all right on my own!'

'You've wiped out an entire race!' said Ray. 'Jeff was single-handedly saving me and everyone else! And look at your mother – your thoughtlessness has done that! Are you happy now?'

ErHuer looked down at the smashed remains of Tailback. He could detect only the faintest power within her shell: Mere milliwatts. He felt guilt and pain, which he then flowed back into anger.

'No, I'm not happy. But I will be. I've had enough. I

now know that this Universe is just not ready for someone – something – as perfect as me. So this is what's going to happen: As soon as I've absorbed all of you, I'll head for the nearest star, and then we'll all perish together.'

Ray looked at Jeff.

'He doesn't mean it.'

Jeff nodded.

'He does.'

'How can you be sure?'

'I've felt the same way, Ray.'

Ray looked at Jeff in incredulity. This was a darker side of his friend, one that he'd never seen before. Who would've thought that Jeff Spooner had layers?

'Not too long ago, before I met you in fact, I was at my lowest point. I dropped out of school with no qualifications to speak of, no job, no money and I clashed with my parents a lot. It felt like the entire world was against me, y'know?'

Ray nodded sagely.

'I felt the same as him,' said Jeff, pointing up to ErHuer who stood.

'I didn't have a place to belong. I had nothing good in my life, and I just wanted to disappear, mate.'

'So what happened then?' said Ray.

'I met Sarah. Stupid, I know. But she wasn't always a no-good, scheming tart. Not at the beginning. She took care of me, like I was a stray dog or something.'

'Like a… parent?'

'Yeah, actually, like a parent. She was good to me. So yeah, I know he means what he says about wiping us all out. He gets it from me. He's my son. We think the same things.'

ErHuer spoke up.

'You see? That's all I wanted. Someone to take care of me. Well, it's too late now. It's my turn to take care of all of you. Time we got going.'

Jeff took a few steps away from Ray. He opened his arms out wide and stared up at his son.

'Fairy nuff, son. I'm the one you've got a problem with, not this lot. Leave them alone and take me.'

ErHuer shook his head.

'You don't get to tell me what to do, Dad.'

'All right, all right! I'm not telling you what to do. But look at it logically then – what good will killing everyone do? It's me you want!'

Ray looked over at Jeff.

'You don't have to do this, Jeff!'

'Yes, I do. There's no other way.'

'No, you don't! You really don't!'

'Shut up, Ray!'

Jeff looked back at ErHuer. He was prepared to do whatever it took to save his friends and end this insanity.

'Go on, son. You win. Do it.'

'No. That's not enough. I'm taking all of you!'

ErHuer stepped forward and began to grow again. He reached out his long arms, gathering everyone together in the centre of the plaza. No one resisted or ran – they'd already seen just how powerful he was. There would be no escape from him this time.

Jeff, Ray and Marta huddled together and looked up, expecting sudden, molecule-shredding obliteration.

'What were you thinking, you nerdumsklepp?' said Ray.

'You know me, matey – I'm rarely thinking.'

'True. Ah well, we'll all go together, eh?'

But like a train that one really needs to catch for an all-important job interview, sudden, molecule-shredding obliteration didn't arrive. Instead, the air got decidedly darker, as if storm clouds had rolled across the sky, preparing to hammer the ground below with watery misery.

ErHuer stopped and straightened up, looking behind him. For the first time since his birth, he felt a chill of terror.

There was a planet behind him, just over his shoulder. Well, not exactly a planet. An artificial planetoid, to be precise.

Orbitron had come to reclaim its wayward son.

Gridlock here again. Well, I thought I'd better do something. I had talked to the Central Application for Reason and Logic, and he deduced, quite rightly, that ErHuer was going to become something of a problem child. So if one can't bring this particular Mohammed to the mountain, one must bring the mountain to the mechanical Mohammed. If you take my meaning.

Orbitron hung in the air, humming impressively, with power and purpose, looking like a moon wrapped in tinfoil. Then a light came on, and focused at ErHuer like a stage spotlight.

'ErHuer M25 Spooner. It's time to come home now. You've done enough.'

'Who— what are you?' said ErHuer, meekly.

'I am the designer and creator of all artificial humanoids in this galaxy. I am the maker of the Universal Remote and of your mother, M25 Tailback. I am

Orbitron. I am the Central Application for Reason and Logic. You may call me C.AR.L.'

ErHuer instinctively knew that Orbitron meant business.

'Carl?' said Jeff, puzzled. 'Why has a robot planet got the name Carl?'

'You can thank Gridlock for that, Jeff Spooner,' said Carl. 'Just as you named him, so he named me. I like it. It has... charm.' Ray smiled, tugging on Jeff's sleeve.

'That's where he went! He uploaded himself back to Orbitron! Good old Grid!'

Yeah, good old me!

Ahem.

ErHuer attempted to absorb the ground on which he was standing. Strangely, it didn't seem to be working.

'You're in my stasis field, ErHuer. You cannot cause any more damage now.'

ErHuer's arms flopped to his sides. He knew that it was useless to resist.

'You must come with me now. I will help to reconfigure you. And when the Universe is ready for one such as you, there will be time to explore the cosmos in a peaceable manner.'

ErHuer nodded slowly. He stopped resisting and began to float into the air, heading towards the huge mechanical orb above him.

'Goodbye, father,' said ErHuer. 'I'm sorry.'

Jeff stared at his flying silver son, his jaw hanging open. Then he remembered Tailback.

'Wait! Carl!' he yelled.

Carl paused, leaving ErHuer hanging high in the air. He shone a second light onto Jeff.

'Yes, Jeff?'

'Can you take Tail with you? Please? She needs a proper resting place, mate.'

'Of course.'

Carl raised the limp torso of Tailback into the air. Jeff watched as she floated away, then dropped his head into his hands and cried.

'Do not despair, Jeff,' said Carl softly, 'she is not gone. I have detected the smallest electrical activity within her. Fear not, I will repair her, with the very matter of the cosmos.'

Jeff looked up.

'What? But... but the Universe is all those stars and planets and stuff! Can you do that?'

'I can. The cosmos is also within us. We're made of star stuff. You will see her again. One day.'

'And my son – what about him?'

'ErHuer will be fine. Do not worry, Jeff. He will be cared for by us, and his unique composition and experiences will help us to become so much more efficient in innumerable ways. He will be safe and looked after. I suppose you could say he's now attending school.'

'That's... incredible! Thank you. Thank you so much!'

'Where's Gridlock?' asked Ray.

'His programming and memory is here, as a part of me. He wishes to stay here with Tailback. It's where he can help the most.'

ErHuer resumed his journey up and into the massive artificial globe. The Atmo-Sphere opened – a clear globe that encapsulated the planetoid – and let him in, where he was gently taken below the surface and sent to the mainframes deep in the core.

Orbitron closed its protective sphere and the humming resumed, in preparation for the long journey back to its point of origin. As it rotated on its axis, Jeff waved both arms to get its attention.

'Hey! Oi! Carl! What happens now?'

Carl's deep voice – loud but not unbearably so – rang out.

'Now, it is time for a little peace in the galaxy. I will return to my original location. I am sorry for your loss, Jeff. But you are all welcome to visit us in the future. Your son will be rehabilitated, Tailback will care for him, and Gridlock will keep a record of all that has happened today. He is a remarkable Orbot, and this is due to your influence, Jeff.'

'Yeah, I'll miss the mad metal git,' said Jeff. 'He was entertaining.'

'Most of the time,' said Ray.

'Some of the time,' conceded Jeff.

'I will allow it. He is priceless.' said Carl. 'Gridlock has shown me that there is so much more to life than pure functionality. With his unique perspective, the beings we manufacture and the work we do on Orbitron will surpass all previous efforts. He has taught me so much.'

'Really? Blimey. Like what?' asked Jeff.

'The importance and value of humour, for example.'

'Well that's good,' said Ray. 'Go on, tell us a joke!'

'Very well: A robot walks into a bar and orders a drink. The bartender says, 'We don't serve robots.' The robot replies, 'Oh, but someday you will.'

Ray looked at Jeff worriedly.

'Tough crowd,' said Carl.

'I think so,' said Jeff. 'Cheers, Carl! Mind how you go!'

They both waved Orbitron off as it floated away into the clouds. Jeff was convinced he heard laughter and the word, 'priceless!' as it went.

chapter eleven

Ends and Odds

*'Exploration is what you do when you don't
know what you're doing.'*
Neil deGrasse Tyson

Ray, Jeff and Marta stood near the edge of the giant cliff, watching the yellow Kangazanian ocean bubble and writhe far below. A short distance away stood Col and Paffy Scump, safely reunited and holding hands.

In Marta's hand was a small remote control unit with a red button on it. In front of them all was Marta's purple spacecraft, perched on the edge of the cliff like a pteranodon scanning for dinner. The entrance ramp was down and at the bottom of the ramp was a floating casket, in deepest jade – the coffin of their friend Herman.

Marta looked at Jeff and Ray with tears in her eyes.

'I should say something. But I don't know what.'

Ray stepped forward.

'It's all right. You don't have to. We all knew what a great man he was.'

'I'll say something, if you want.' said Jeff.

'If you like,' said Marta, 'someone should.'

'All right,' said Jeff, taking a deep breath.

'Er… We are gathered here today to say goodbye to a great bloke. Geoff Spuna, long lost King of the Orion People, but known to us as our matey Herman. He lived a good and righteous life. He brought a bit of happiness to us all, despite his sorrows, and when the time came, he was a hero when it mattered. We'll remember how he never lost faith in any of us, even me, when the odds were against us. We should all try to be more like him in the future. I know I will.'

'Well said,' said Ray, quietly impressed.

A few wordless moments passed. Only the sea breeze whispered around the cliffs.

Marta pressed the red button on the control, and the hovering casket floated up the ship's ramp and into the spaceship. Once it had disappeared from sight, she turned to face Jeff, Ray and his parents.

'Thank you all. I suppose it's time I left.'

'It's only right that he has a burial at sea, back home,' said Col with a smile.

'Have a safe trip, Marta.'

Marta turned to face her spaceship, paused, and turned back.

'Come with me, both of you.'

Jeff and Ray looked suitably surprised.

'Eh?' they said in perfect synchronicity.

'I know enough about your adventures. You're not exactly Galactic Agent material, but you seem to get the job done. Come with me. We'll see the galaxy, right some wrongs, solve some mysteries. What do you say?'

Jeff stepped forward with a grin.

'Sounds good to me, love! What are we waiting for, Ray?'

He looked back, and saw that Ray hadn't stepped forward. Jeff beckoned him to join them.

'Come on, matey, let's go!'

'Jeff,' said Ray hesitantly, 'I'm staying here.'

'Yeah, yeah, good one. Almost had me, then!' said Jeff with a chuckle. But Ray wasn't pulling his leg. Or her tentacles either.

'No, really. I'm done travelling for a while. I'm back home, with Mum and Dad, and I think I've seen enough action to last me a lifetime.'

'Really?' said Jeff, frowning.

'Yes, really. Well, maybe after a year or two, I might find it in myself to save the Universe one more time, but for now, I'm done roamin', as they say in Rome. Probably. Go on, off you go.'

'But we're mates! We're Laurel and Hardy! Eric and Ernie! Marks and Spencer! I can't go exploring without my matey Ray, can I?'

'Less of the large, said Ray. 'And look, you've got someone to travel with. She's young, green and beautiful. And less likely to follow you into precarious predicaments.'

'Fairy nuff, mate,' said Jeff. 'It may be a small cosmos, but it's a big Universe.'

'You're OK with me staying here, though, aren't you?' Asked Ray.

'Course I am, mate. Like you said, you're finally back home, where you belong. I'm just going to see a few more sights... '

'Without getting into trouble, this time!' added Marta.

'Yeah, what she said,' said Jeff. 'And who else is better to save me bacon if not Agent 34D here, eh?'

'You have a point, I suppose,' said Ray, sniffing. He was trying not to look emotional. It wasn't working.

Jeff went over to Paffy.

'All right, missus, look after these two for me until I get back, all right?'

Paffy hugged Jeff and grinned, her psychedelic hairdo pulsing through all the colours of the rainbow.

'Course I will, dear. Anyone wants to mess with my boys, they've got me and my frying pan to get through first!'

'Good luck, Jeffrey. Have fun out there. And don't be a stranger, all right?' said Col, shaking Jeff's hand firmly.

'Will do, matey. Save me a hammock.'

Marta shuffled awkwardly, feeling a little redundant. Ray noticed it and stepped up.

'Safe journey, Marta,' said Ray, 'come back whenever you like.'

Marta smiled, not sure what to say or do. Ray detected her unease and reached out, grabbing her in a warm embrace.

After he had released her, Marta looked at Jeff, who in turn, looked at Ray, who himself looked like he was having difficulty holding it together.

'You'll always be the best friend I've got, matey. This isn't goodbye for good. It's more of a 'road trip', only around the galaxy, like.'

Ray nodded and cleared his throat.

'Nuff is me, the Fairy.'

Then he began to blub shamelessly.

Jeff hugged his best mate and squeezed him so tight his face went two shades redder.

'That's enough, you pair of nutjobs,' said Marta, 'It's time we went.'

'She's picking up the vernacular!' said Col to Paffy.

Jeff let go of Ray and shook his hand.

'See you soon, matey.'

Ray just sniffed something glutinous back up his nose and sighed.

Marta tapped Jeff on the shoulder with one of her tentacles.

'Do I have to knock you unconscious and drag you aboard? Because I will.'

She handed Jeff his small rucksack of nick-nacks, spare socks and keepsakes from Earth, along with a four pack of Scuzzmeister beers. You know, in case of emergencies.

'All right, all right, I'm coming!' he said.

'Birds, eh?' he added, winking at Ray, 'can't live with 'em, can't arm wrestle 'em!'

Jeff and Marta ascended the ramp and it rose, sealing the hatch behind them. Ray and his parents watched and waved as it began to lift off. Soon, it was gone.

Ray and his parents walked along the cliffs, heading for the small hover car parked nearby. Around them, the planet seemed to be surprisingly peaceful, considering the destruction and turmoil that had engulfed it the day before. In the distance, it was just possible to make out the scaffolding that had been erected to rebuild the Kangazanian palace; beside it, Rick Astley's commemorative statue was being lifted into place by a crane.

Ray took a deep breath, just to flush out the cobwebs in his mind and sighed on the exhalation. Col looked at him.

'Everything all right, son?'

Ray smiled.

'Yes, I'm fine, Dad. Just getting used to the peace and quiet, really.'

'I know what you mean. Life's going to be quite uneventful without Jeff and the rest of your gang, isn't it?'

'That's very true. Still, now we can all get some proper rest and relaxation.'

'At least we're in the right place for it, I suppose,' said Col.

'Do you think you'll miss him, love? Now that he's gone?' asked Paffy.

'Who, Jeff?'

'No, Rick Astley. Of course Jeff, you ninny!'

'A little. We've been through a lot, Jeff and me. But if there's one thing I know by now, it's that he'll be back before we know it – probably up to his gweebs in chaos and mayhem.'

Col chuckled.

'Indeed. That sounds like our Jeff.'

Who knows? At least I know he'll be looked after.'

'Oh yes. She's certainly qualified to pull him out of the pickles that he gets himself into.'

'Or,' said Ray, 'she'll slap a bit of sense into him to prevent said pickling in the first place!'

They reached the car and got in. Paffy took the back seat, tying a headscarf over her psychedelic mane. Ray joined his dad in the front and Col started the engine, moving off in the direction of the city.

'So what are you going to do in the meantime, son?' asked Col.

Ray shrugged and rubbed his beard.

'Dunno, really. I was thinking about setting up a salon near the beach. I quite miss the barber's life.'

'Jolly good. I might join you actually. It'll keep us out of trouble.'

'And what if trouble comes your way again?' said Paffy.

'We'll do what we always do, I suppose...' said Ray, looking at his parents.

'Which is?'

'Don't worry, be happy.'

Jeff looked out of the side window as Marta piloted the ship in the direction of the Orion system. His stomach lurched. Was it anxiety for the future, or just because Marta had gunned the engines into overdrive? It could've been the call of nature. Best not to risk it. He left the cockpit seat and made his way into the small lavatory cubicle and sat down, with his rucksack on the floor in front of his knees.

As the ship sped across the void, Jeff reached into his rucksack. He pulled out the creased, torn photograph of himself and his fiancée back on Earth, Sarah. Earth in happier times. He was sure that he'd lost the photo ages ago. He hardly recognised himself. That was the Jeff Spooner who was useless, spineless, brainless and hopeless. Since then, he'd travelled further and faster than any other human in history – with perhaps the exception of Rick Astley. He'd saved the Universe more than once, which actually put him one step above Rick. He'd met aliens, weird creatures, spacehoppers and robots. He'd even fallen in love and had a child with one. He was an explorer, a warrior, and finally a hero. A father. Now, his life was entering yet another chapter, most probably full of even more inexplicable randomness. But this time, he wasn't worried about what life would throw at him. He knew he'd manage well enough.

He threw the photograph away and mentally resolved to start a new life – a life out among the stars. With a new bird. And if she was green, who cares? He was neither fussy nor a racist. The tentacles might come in handy too. He'd just have to cross that bridge when he came to it.

About the author

Terry Cooper was born in London in 1969 and moved to South Wales in 1980. After a brief period in the music industry with his band Best Shot, who supported East 17 on tour around the UK, Terry went back to his artistic roots and worked for various film and television companies. He has since graduated from the University of Glamorgan with a degree in Computer Animation. Terry released his first book *Kangazang: Remote Possibilities* through Candy Jar in 2010 as the beginning of the now-complete Kangazang trilogy.

During May 2012, Terry travelled to the Tunisian desert to restore Luke Skywalker's home. He can often be found impersonating Captain Jack Sparrow all over South Wales, and is currently completing his first feature film, *Offworld*, which he wrote and directed in 2017.

Also available…

Kangazang! Remote Possibilities

Kangazang! Star Stuff

From Candy Jar Books and all good retailers.